LIGHT TRAVELER
Adventure Series
Book One

My Body Fell Off!

LIGHT TRAVELER ADVENTURE SERIES

My Body Fell Off!

Silver Hawk's Revenge

Missing Children

LIGHT TRAVELER
Adventure Series

Book One

My Body Fell Off!

a novel

BJ ROWLEY

GoldenWings

This is a work of fiction, and the events in this book are not intended as doctrinal statements or beliefs. The views expressed herein are the sole responsibility of the author. Likewise, characters, places, and incidents are either the product of the author's imagination or are represented fictitiously, and any resemblance to actual persons, living or dead, or actual events or locales, is entirely coincidental.

My Body Fell Off!

Published by Golden Wings Enterprises
P.O. Box 468, Orem, Utah 84059-0468

GoldenWings is a registered trademark of Golden Wings Enterprises.

ISBN 0-9700103-1-1

Printed in the United States of America
Year of first printing, current edition: 2000

10 9 8 7 6 5 4 3 2 1

For my wife and children,
who endured patiently while I continually
monopolized the computer.

Special thanks to Scott Gurney of the Orem City Fire Department,
and his wife, Cheryl, for their technical expertise.
Also to Craig and Ange Holland, for their boundless enthusiasm
and their invaluable feedback and editing skills.

For all have not every gift given unto them;
for there are many gifts,
and to every man is given a gift
by the Spirit of God.

PROLOGUE

The first time it happened, I was in third grade. I had been recuperating in the hospital after having my appendix removed. They had me all drugged up on painkillers, and I was feeling really goofy, so, at the time, I passed it off as just a weird dream. I thought about the "dream" on and off for several weeks after that, but eventually it slipped into oblivion and was forgotten.

The second time it happened was two years later. Our school class was on an overnight camping trip for fifth graders. We were hiking in the dark, around midnight—no flashlights allowed and no talking. (Our leaders thought it would give us a better appreciation for nature or something—I'm not sure.) Anyway, I lost my footing climbing down a little hill and slipped several feet into a steep ravine. I landed headfirst against a big rock and was knocked cold for a couple of minutes. My friends said later that when I finally got up, I babbled and carried on, saying all kinds of stupid things. I don't remember any of that. The weirdness happened later, while I was lying in the back of the ambulance. It was like . . . floating and drifting and moving up and down.

As it turned out, I had fractured my skull right above the left temple. After a weeklong stay in the hospital, I was sent home. By then, I was sure that I had suffered permanent brain damage and would be retarded for the rest of my life. Eventually the headaches went away, and I came to realize that I was still the same old me. Again, the whole incident passed from my mind and was forgotten.

The third time it happened, I still didn't recognize the gift for what it was. I had just started my sophomore year in high school . . . and I thought for sure I was dead . . .

CHAPTER 1

- *Utah* -

The big day finally arrived! I was in High School! Tenth Grade! The only problem was, I wasn't in California, where I was supposed to be. I was in Payson, Utah, of all places. Like . . . Siberia!

Just one month earlier, my dad had popped the surprise of the century on us at the dinner table. "Guess what, everybody!" he had announced with a big cheesy grin. "We're moving to Utah!"

Just like that. Clean out of the blue. No warning at all.

I couldn't believe my ears. "This is a joke, right, Dad?" I choked out with a forced laugh. I knew it wasn't.

"Nope. No joke. We're moving to Utah."

I leaped to my feet. "But Dad, school starts in a month. I've been waiting all my life for high school, and now we're moving to . . . to . . . to Utah?" It was like bitter poison dripping off my tongue. "Why?" I asked in a pleading tone.

"Because I've been promoted," he announced proudly, "and I've been given a special assignment to open up our new office in Utah Valley and help get things going over there."

How could they do that to me? Just when life was really getting fun. I was only five weeks away from turning sixteen. Five weeks from finally reaching our family's officially sanctioned dating age. Five weeks—thirty-five days—until I would finally start dating all those gorgeous California girls—dances, beach parties, concerts!

In Utah, the girls will all be . . . farmers! I thought. *HOW DISGUSTING!*

Not to mention that I was right smack dab in the middle of Driver's Ed. Only one measly month away from becoming a licensed driver.

In Utah, they probably all drive around on tractors or something!

The very next day, Dad had flown right out and found us a house. A huge two-story monstrosity out in the middle of nowhere. Nothing but farms as far as the eye could see. Dad said he had endured the crowded neighborhoods long enough, and he went out of his way to find something rural. Our closest neighbor was about two hundred yards away. We didn't really even live in Payson. We were three miles from town, on the West Mountain road.

The only good thing about the move was that I finally got my own bedroom. I had been sharing with my obnoxious little brother, Darin "the dweeb," since the beginning of time. In our new house, even the two little brats, Charlene and Cynthia, had their own rooms.

Of course, not having Chris around anymore helped. My older brother was definitely what you would call the black sheep of our family. (Mom would have grounded me for a week, though, if she ever heard me say that.)

"We need to pour out our love for him," she would tell us. "He'll turn around someday."

"He's a good spirit deep down inside," Dad would add. "He just needs some time."

Well, if there was a good spirit in there, it was waaaaay too deep for me to find it. Chris had been in more trouble than anybody I knew. It was a wonder he hadn't already been given life in prison.

Now, that's a pleasant thought.

Anyway, Chris had laid it on the line with my folks and refused to leave California. So, we left him.

We were supposed to ride a bus to school, but we didn't know when or where, so Mom drove us the first day. I was dropped off first, since the high school started earlier. Darin and the girls looked like they were about to face a firing squad when they drove off.

As I walked in the front doors, I heard someone call my name.

"Hey, Bart. That IS your name, right? Bart?"

I nodded. I recognized him from our first church meeting on Sunday, and he reminded me that his name was Paul Bishop.

"So, what do you think of Utah so far?" he asked.

"Well, I expected everybody to be wearing cowboy hats and boots and stuff. I guess I wasn't very well informed," I answered.

Paul laughed. "Well, don't worry. There are plenty of them around. So, where's your first class?"

I told him I hadn't picked up my schedule yet. Mom had come in the day before and got me registered, so I was still in the dark. He guided me to the office and waited while I got my papers and locker assignment. I couldn't make any sense of the schedule and finally lowered my pride enough to ask him for help.

"Yeah, it's kind of confusing," he said. "It's like college. My sister Diane was a junior last year, so we're pretty used to it now." He explained that a "module" was a forty-minute block of time, like from eight to eight-forty. There was a ten-minute break after each module. Most classes were one module, five days a week, like a regular period. Others were only on Monday, Wednesday and Friday, or on Tuesday and Thursday.

"Then there's one module of study time each day," he continued. "There are a bunch of study halls where you can go, like the library or the cafeteria. But you can't just wander the halls. Hey, look," he said, reading my schedule. "We have study hall at the same time."

By that time we had arrived at Paul's locker, and he busied himself working the lock and stashing his things.

"Where's your locker?" he asked.

I looked at the papers. "Umm . . . two thirty-three. Where's that?"

"Right down this same hall, I think."

Paul seemed like an all right guy, and I was relieved that I didn't have to find everything on my own. We found my locker at the end of the hall—the very last locker in the farthest corner of the school.

"Hey, at least you don't have to bump shoulders with anyone on the left," he said, trying to cheer me up.

The lock was stubborn, and when I finally got the door opened I accidentally backed into someone on my right. I turned to find myself looking down into the clearest, crystal blue eyes I had ever seen in my life. I stepped back a foot and stood there speechless, staring shamelessly.

This gorgeous creature is definitely NOT a farm girl, I thought.

Her face was so perfect, she looked like she could easily have been a model for *Seventeen* magazine. She had incredibly long, wavy blond hair that went clear down to her waist—what little waist there was. She could have been straight off a California beach . . . except without a suntan.

"Aren't you even going to say 'excuse me'?" she asked, pretending to be upset. Her voice was soft and sensuous.

"Uh . . . oh . . . excuse me," I stammered, clearing my throat. She smiled and winked.

I just about died. My adrenaline went to red alert status. *What a stupid first impression THAT was,* I thought. I turned back to face Paul, totally embarrassed. He raised his eyebrows at me a couple of times and made a little hourglass gesture with his hands.

Paul told me later that her name was Tiffany Short, and that she was a junior varsity cheerleader.

"Her friends call her Tiff—or Shorty. But I wouldn't, if I were you. Definitely one hot babe. You don't stand a chance with her, though. She's Tom Zeller's girlfriend. He's our quarterback—the big number fourteen. You better keep your distance."

The rest of the day was a pretty typical first day of school. It turned out that Paul and I had two classes together; English and history. My homeroom class was geometry. The rest of my classes included tech crew, P.E., and biology. The tech crew was in charge of the auditorium for all assemblies and productions, and the class was two hours long, on Tuesdays and Thursdays.

On Friday, I had my first run-in with the rednecks. I had inadvertently stepped in front of them in the hall as I left my locker. There were four of them, all decked out in hats and boots and big shiny belt buckles. I half expected to see spurs and six-shooters.

One of them stuck his thumbs in his belt and said, "Well, lookie here. We got ourselves a new little runt in the pen. What do we do with runts, boys?"

The other three cowboys laughed and mumbled some things I didn't catch.

The big shot took a step forward and poked me hard in the chest with his finger. His eyes narrowed. "You even know what a runt is, kid?" Before I could begin to answer, he enlightened me. "Runts are little itty bitty squealy pigs that never grow up. All the rest get big and fat, but the runts just stay little." He paused, tipping his head back and raising his hat. "You know what happens to the runts?" he asked.

"No. What?" I knew it couldn't be anything good, whatever it was.

"The big pigs kill 'em!" he roared, stomping the floor with the heel of his boot. "They tromp 'em to death!" They all laughed and slapped each other on their backs and shoulders. "That's what we're going to do to you, runt, if you ever get in our way again. You can just think of us as the Big Pigs. Got it?"

"Yeah, I got it," I muttered.

With that, he shoved me against the lockers and out of the way. Then they paraded on down the hall in their exaggerated bow-legged strut.

"Big Pigs is right," I said under my breath.

On the way home, on the bus, I told Paul about my run-in.

He explained, "There are three kinds of guys in this school: the jocks, the rednecks, and the rest of us. This is the FFA capital of Utah. That's Future Farmers of America," he said sarcastically. "They have more sheep shearing classes here than they have reading, writing, and arithmetic all put together." We both laughed.

I sat quietly for a minute or two, watching the cornfields through the window.

"So, why did they pick me, out of hundreds of sophomores?" I wondered out loud.

"Hey, we only have one high school and one junior high in this town," Paul answered. "These are the same guys that have been harassing us since kindergarten. They just get meaner as they get older. You're a new face. You stick out like a sore thumb—ripe for the pickins."

I told myself that I would need to remember that in the future. I was an invader.

"Nothing personal, Bart," Paul said.

"Yeah, I know."

"Don't ever underestimate those guys, though," he warned. "Last year they beat up a long-haired hippy-looking guy that moved in from Illinois. Sent him to the hospital all broken to pieces."

The rest of the ride home passed in silence.

So, this is Utah, I thought. *Cowboy heaven.*

CHAPTER 2

- Roshayne -

During the next couple of days, I reached the milestones that I had been waiting for all my life. And they were the most miserably uneventful events imaginable.

Saturday I turned sixteen. My party consisted of cake and ice cream, and five minutes of opening presents from my family. Big wow. All I could think about was the big beach party my California friends would have been having for me. And Tuesday I aced the driving test and finally became a licensed driver—and couldn't even show off to anybody. Another big wow.

The next few days of school went smoothly enough. By the end of the first week, I had the place figured out and could get from one class to the next without getting lost or being tardy. I also figured out which ways to go and not to go, to avoid running into the Big Pigs.

I only saw Tiffany at her locker twice. I said "Hi" both times, but she basically just ignored me. Anyplace else I saw her, she was glued to Mr. Football.

The class that turned out to be a big surprise was tech crew. I had no idea how much fun running an auditorium could be. All of the lighting and sound equipment were state-of-the-art and practically new. I was assigned to the light crew; we were in charge of setting lights, running the spots, and controlling the light board. There was also a sound crew in charge of the microphones and sound equipment, and a back stage crew in charge of props, sets, and curtains. We each had a complete set of keys, so I had access anytime I wanted.

Friday I invited Paul on a tour. We entered the auditorium through one of the double doors in the back, just off the main hall.

"Gee, this is awesome," he said, casting his gaze around the empty auditorium. His words echoed back and he continued in a whisper, "Are you sure we won't get in trouble for being here?"

"I have my own keys," I assured him. "We can let ourselves in anytime we want."

"So what do you do in here?"

"I haven't had time to really do much yet. I was thinking that we could put on some cool music and throw a light show for ourselves."

"Yeah, that would be cool."

"I'll give you the guided tour as we go."

Twenty feet to our left, through a gap in the back row of seats, was our first stop. I produced a key and we entered the sound room.

"This is where the sound manager runs the mikes and plays music," I told him in my best tour guide voice. "This unit here is for the headphones, so we can all talk to each other during a production."

We found a tape with the last year's top one hundred hits on it and piped it out softly over the speaker system. Next I took him up on the stage and showed him how the fly system worked. "All the curtains and lights and sets can be raised up into the ceiling with these ropes back here," I explained.

"It looks twice as big, wide open like this," he observed.

I pointed out the trap door in the middle of the floor that dropped into the basement, and the orchestra pit in front of the stage.

"Now for the fun part," I said, pointing to the seemingly endless flight of stairs on the side wall.

"Where does that go?"

"To the light room in the ceiling," I answered, already on the tenth step, "where the spotlights are—and the control board."

We were both a little winded by the time we finally got to the top. Passing through the doorway was like walking into a fantasy world. As far as we could see in the semi-darkness was a vast maze of wooden catwalks, suspended by heavy cables and leading off in all directions. Heat vents snaked around everywhere, covered by sprayed-on yellow foam insulation. Wires were strung haphazardly overhead, like a giant spider web.

The catwalks swayed back and forth and squeaked in protest as we maneuvered our way toward the back. Every one in a while we had to duck under girder beams or climb over pipes that crossed the walkway. Finally we came to a door and a wall, right in the middle of the attic. The light room was a full fifteen by thirty feet, all finished off and modern looking. Only the lower two feet of the room actually hung down below the auditorium ceiling.

"I had no idea this was up here," Paul said in awe. We turned on two of the spotlights and played tag with them on the stage floor.

Finally, I introduced Paul to the control board.

"It looks like something out of Star Trek," he said.

We experimented with all the colored lights for a while, treating ourselves to a pretty decent light show.

All of a sudden, Paul looked at his watch and yelled, "Oh, no! We're late!" We shut everything down in a mad rush and bounded noisily back through the catwalks and down the stairs. Then we raced up the isle and rammed open the panic bars on the exit doors.

When we charged out into the hall from the darkened auditorium, we were both blinded temporarily by the bright light. We squinted, shielded our eyes with our hands—and ran head-on into three girls coming toward us. All three of them screamed bloody murder, while books and papers went flying in all directions. One was knocked backwards to the floor. The other two lit into us in a violent rage.

"Why don't you watch where you're going?! You're gonna kill somebody!" the first one exploded, finishing it off with a long string of profanities.

"Look at my stuff! It's everywhere!" screamed the second. She was livid. "We're going to be late for class!" She went down on all fours and started wildly gathering up papers and folders.

"Great! You broke my nail!" cried the foul-mouthed one, holding her fingers up for my inspection. "You're gonna pay for this!"

I started scrambling around, trying to help pick things up.

"Don't touch my stuff!" snapped the second one, grabbing her purse out of my hand. "Don't you think you've done enough damage already? Get lost!"

I backed up awkwardly and stood with my hands in my back pockets, not knowing what else to do. The third girl was still sitting on the floor, her hair hanging down over her face. She held one hand to her chest, trying to catch her breath. Paul went over and hauled her to her feet.

"I'm sorry, Rosh. We didn't see you coming," Paul said. "Are you okay?"

She didn't say anything—just gave us the evil eye and proceeded to gather up her things. We backed off a ways farther.

"You know her?" I asked Paul in a whisper.

"Sure. She goes to our church. Come on. Let's get out of here. We're going to be late."

We took off at a dead run without looking back.

Our next class was history. We were late, but nobody seemed to notice. The whole class was on its feet reciting the Gettysburg Address, or some such thing. I slipped quietly over to my desk. Paul did the same. Since I didn't know exactly what was going on, I decided to occupy my time looking around at the girls. I was surprised to realize that, after two weeks of school, the only two girls that I recognized were the two sitting directly to the side of me. Both very good looking, coincidentally. I decided to take a good look at the rest of the girls in the class, to "find some good in everyone," as Mom always told us.

That one has nice hair, I thought. Then, looking at the next, *She's got cute dimples when she says certain words.* On to the next. *Sorta cute, I guess.*

Just then, I heard a girl's giggle somewhere behind me during a pause in the recitation. Not a little-girl giggle, but a unique, soft little chuckle that went up the scale a bit at the end. It was captivating. I spun around to find the source.

And there she was.

Her eyes caught mine for a fraction of a second, then went back to her friend. I might as well have stuck my finger in an electrical outlet. That split second of eye contact raised the hair on the back of my neck and sent goose bumps all up and down. She was stunning. Her face was bursting with the most beautiful smile I had ever seen in my life. Of course, I knew the smile wasn't meant for me, but I imagined it was. Guys would do almost anything for a smile like that. Time seemed to stop. Heaven couldn't have been any better than that brief moment.

Without thinking, I instantly and automatically smiled back.

Another fraction of a second later and her eyes were back, locked onto mine like a laser beam.

I suddenly recognized who she was.

One of the girls we just ran down in the hall, I realized. *The one that fell down! She must have come in right behind us.*

Her smile disappeared, like turning off a light. Mine faded with it. At first she looked surprised. That changed instantly to annoyed. Surely she recognized me for the jerk that I was. When I didn't look away, her expression changed to mild amusement, then to deep consternation as she tried to figure me out. After that, it changed briefly to timidity as my stare bore into her.

But she still didn't look away. Our eyes seemed to be locked together by some invisible force. Finally her brows furrowed, and she turned studious. Neither of us dared to blink or breathe. I memorized every minute detail of her features. Her Latin eyes—dark brown with a few orange specks. Her long eyelashes with a hint of blue eye shadow. The thick bangs that covered her forehead and hung down to her eyebrows. Her dainty little shiny lips, and that small, cute-looking nose.

I wanted to see what the rest of her looked like, but didn't dare while she was staring at me like that. After a few seconds, it seemed as if she was looking right through me—right into my very center. My heart skipped a few beats, and my knees felt weak. It was almost like she was reading my mind.

Still, I couldn't break away. Nor could she. Man, it was the greatest! I wanted to gaze into those mysterious brown eyes forever. An indescribable tingling sensation came over me that I had never felt before.

"Excuse me. Mister Elderberry? Miss Pennini?"

The sound of my own name broke the spell. As I spun around, I was shocked to find that we were the only ones still standing. Whatever they had been reciting was long over, and there was a guy standing at the front with a paper in his hands, ready to read something to the class. Everyone was staring at us.

The teacher, Mr. Bell continued, "Would you two lovebirds care to join us?"

The whole class burst into laughter. We sat down quickly.

I could just die.

I'm sure Mr. Bell gave his usual dynamic presentation that day, but I never heard a word. My mind was in a whirlwind.

Who is she? What did Paul say her name was? Tish? Tosh? Something weird. Why did she look at me like that? I smiled. *Maybe she likes me!* I frowned. *That's stupid. Why would she? I just creamed her in the hall. She probably hates my guts.*

I tried to steal a glance or two at her during class, but she seemed absorbed in something on her desk and never looked up. I was still trying to regain my composure when the bell rang. She exited the room like a bolt of lightning, while I got caught up in the crowd. By the time I finally pushed my way out the door, she was disappearing down the hall and out of the building.

Later, on the bus, I was introduced to a couple of Paul's friends by the names of Neil McBride and Scott Norton. "Neil just turned sixteen and got his driver's license a couple of days ago," Paul informed me. Neil beamed proudly from ear to ear. "That makes him The Most Likely to Succeed as our Chauffeur."

"That is, if I can talk my parents out of a car," Neil conceded.

"I just got mine, too," I said. "And there's always my dad's old pickup truck."

We talked about cars and driving for a while. Finally I got up the nerve and asked, "Hey, Paul, what did you say that girl's name was? The one we knocked down?"

He looked at me quizzically. "Rosh," he said. "Actually it's Roshayne. Roshayne Pennini. She lives just west of where the tracks cross the highway. Why?"

"Roshayne Pennini." I sat back, drinking in the name like a glass of cold water, repeating it to myself several times and committing it to memory.

Paul grinned. "Hey, you got the hots for her?"

"No!" I denied, a little too quickly. "Just wondering, that's all."

"So what was that little scene in history today?"

"She . . . uh . . . was mad at me . . . for what happened in the hall," I stammered.

"Yeah, whatever."

CHAPTER 3

- The Gift -

I woke up slowly Sunday morning and had to concentrate for a couple of minutes to figure out what day it was.

Sunday, I realized, closing my eyes and relaxing. *I can sleep another hour or so.*

That didn't happen, though. Mom had to be at church early for some dumb meeting, and since the chapel was over three miles away, we all had to go together at the same time.

As soon as we arrived, Mom headed off down the long hall, and Dad disappeared with some men into an office. Darin and the girls did their own disappearing acts, leaving me alone in the foyer.

I sank down into one of the sofas and occupied my time trying to read the various notices on the bulletin board from fifteen feet away. Dad sometimes called me "Eagle Eyes" because of my ability to see things so much sooner and better than everyone else.

I was squinting hard and right in the middle of reading about the youth dance that was going to be held that coming Saturday, when my line of vision was blocked by a little old lady moving at a snail's pace through the foyer. She looked like she had to be at least a hundred and ninety years old. She was all hunched over and leaning on one of those walker things with wheels. Just when I thought she would finally clear the way, she stopped, looked all around like she was lost, and finally looked in my general direction. Then her eyes landed on me and her eyebrows furrowed. She stared holes right through me for several seconds. It made me feel sort of creepy, and I stood up to try to get out from under her steady gaze.

But she kept me firmly locked in. Carefully, she hobbled up to me and grabbed my left hand in hers, never once releasing me from her piercing stare. She had to strain her neck to look up at my face.

"My boy," she said, in her frail and squeaky voice, "You are one of God's special ones. I know it. I can see it in your eyes. I can feel it, just being close to you. Touching your hand makes me tingle from top to bottom. Do you know why?" Before I could respond, she pulled me down close and whispered in my ear, "You have a gift, you know. A very special gift."

Having eagle eyes is a gift? I questioned silently.

"I don't know exactly what it is," she continued, "but the Spirit bore witness very strongly to me just now that you are special. The Lord has given you something very precious and extremely rare. You will be a great blessing to many people, if you are humble and use it wisely. If you are selfish or use it thoughtlessly, the Lord will withdraw it from you. Be strong." With that she drew away, and her voice returned to normal. "Thank you, son. And bless you."

And she left.

I just stood there with my mouth hanging open. I didn't know what to say.

What did she mean, 'You have a gift'? I asked myself. *Something precious and rare? Give me a break.* My only immediate knowledge of spiritual gifts consisted of the gift of tongues, and nothing else.

I don't even know anybody who doesn't speak English. Why on earth would God give me a gift like that? I was flabbergasted. *What's he expecting me to do with it?*

She made it all sound so ominous and sacred. I had never considered myself an evil person, but I sure didn't look at myself as someone God would treat in any special way.

An hour or so later, Paul and I were sitting together in Sunday School class. I pretended to listen to the lesson for a few minutes, but I couldn't get the old lady's words off my mind.

Paul sensed my mood and whispered, "Hey, man. What's up? You look like you've seen a ghost or something."

I whispered back, "Do you know that old woman who walks around with the walker? Really old and hunched over?"

"Ol' Lady Owens? Of course. Who doesn't?" he whispered.

"Well," I explained, "she came up to me in the foyer before church and told me she had a revelation or a vision or something about God giving me a special gift. Is that weird, or what?"

Paul's eyes lit up. "She told you that?"

"Yeah, why?"

"Did she tell you what the gift was?"

"No. She said she didn't know. But she was sure convinced that it was something . . . what did she say? . . . 'rare and precious' or something like that."

"No way!" he said, a little too loudly.

"Would you two mind saving whatever it is you're doing for after class, please?" said the teacher. We were obedient for a while, until he turned his back to write on the chalkboard.

Paul leaned over and whispered, "Ol' Lady Owens is practically a prophet around here, Bart. She has visions and stuff all the time. And they ALWAYS come true."

"You're kidding."

"Serious. Two years ago she told my dad that if he didn't hurry and make peace with his father, it would be too late. Three days later, my grandpa died of a heart attack. My dad has been sick about that ever since, for not calling him and talking to him."

"Gosh."

"Then one time, she told Mister Palmer how sorry she was that he was having money problems. He didn't know what she was talking about. The very next day we had a real bad storm that laid his entire wheat crop on the ground. He had to go on welfare."

"Holy cow," I whispered.

Paul was quiet for a second, searching his memory. "Another time she—"

"Shh!" I stopped him. Something the teacher had just said caught my attention.

" . . . 'for there are many gifts, and to every man is given a gift by the Spirit of God'," quoted the teacher, his scriptures open in his hand. He looked up at the class and explained, "And then there's a long list of gifts covered in the next several verses, like the gift of tongues and so forth. Then we jump to verse twenty-six. It says, 'And all these gifts come from God, for the benefit of the children of God.'" Then he continued on with his discussion.

I felt goose bumps all over my arms.

What a coincidence, I thought. *Ol' Lady Owens, and now this?* Then I remembered something Dad had taught us once. "There's no such thing as a coincidence," he said. "Everything is known to God, from the beginning to the end. If a coincidence happens, you can be sure God caused it, for one reason or another."

I rubbed my arms. *But, why?* I asked myself. *And what?*

CHAPTER 4

- The Freeze -

Another week came and went before I knew it. I had been watching for Roshayne all day every day, but I only caught an occasional glimpse of her in history and once in the library during study hall. She steadfastly ignored my attempts to establish eye contact.

Tiffany, on the other hand, finally said "Hi" once. She even smiled at me. Talk about a heart stopper.

On Saturday, Paul invited me over to his house, and I succeeded in talking my dad out of the truck. Paul introduced me to his mother, then we hung out in his bedroom for the rest of the afternoon. We also planned to check out the church youth dance later that night.

His "room" looked more like an abandoned TV repair shop than a place where somebody sleeps. It was huge and was littered from corner to corner with all kinds of contraptions and inventions. Dozens of do-it-yourself electronics kits and radio sets. Years' worth of worn out or half finished science experiments. Shelves full of technical reference books.

Boy, this guy is really a science freak, I concluded.

What caught my eye was the model airplane on his desk.

"It's an RC kit," he explained. "I've been putting it together all summer, and I'm almost finished."

"How do you fly it?" I asked. "Around in circles on a long cord?" The only remote control planes I had ever seen were the kiddie versions from Toys-R-Us.

"No, it's radio controlled." He showed me the hand-held controller. "See these levers and knobs? They're basically the same as the ones in a real airplane." Paul proceeded to show me all the literature and photos that came with the kit. He even started up the motor for a few minutes, but it made a ton of noise and smoked up the bedroom.

We got so engrossed in his projects that we both forgot about the dance until his mom came up to ask me if I needed a ride.

"Holy cow!" I exclaimed, looking at my watch. "It starts in five minutes."

I pushed that poor old truck to its limits getting home. Supper consisted of a fast grilled cheese sandwich and a glass of milk. I took a record-speed shower and was just putting on my shoes when Paul's car pulled up.

Mom HAD to go out and meet him and his mom, of course. Not because we were new in the area or anything, but mostly just to "casually" mention our curfew rules.

"Tomorrow is Sunday, remember," she admonished, pointing her finger at me. "You need to leave the dance by eleven-thirty. I don't want you out after midnight."

Moms could sure be a pain sometimes.

The dance was held in the church house in town, and was well under way by the time we got there. We found Scott and Neil hanging out by the refreshment table, watching the girls.

"How long you been here?' Paul asked.

"A couple of minutes, is all," answered Scott. "We're just starting to case the joint." We all filled napkins to overflowing with cookies and started looking for a table we could share with someone.

"Hey, that looks like Jill over there, with Tammy and someone else," Neil said, pointing to a table across the room. We followed him as he blazed a trail through the crowded recreation hall. It took a circus-style balancing act for me to keep my punch and cookies intact the whole way.

"Mind if we join you?" asked Neil politely as he sat down next to the perky looking blonde on the right.

"Well, hi there!" she exclaimed. She lit up like a light bulb. It was obvious they were an item already. Paul sat down next to the brunette on the left. Scott and I pulled up chairs on the other side of the table, facing the girl in the middle.

I froze in midair, hovering three inches above my seat, when I realized that the "someone else" was none other than Roshayne

Pennini. My heart stopped.

"Roshayne Pennini!" I blurted out, before I could stop myself. She blushed and looked down at her lap as I settled into my chair.

"Oh, you two met already?" Neil asked.

Paul laughed. "Yeah, they met all right. In a head-on collision a week ago."

"In a crash?" the blonde gasped.

"Not in cars," he explained quickly. "They literally RAN into each other."

"You were there, too. Remember?" I said. "In fact, you were the one who ran into her. I hit the other two."

He shrugged and rattled off the juicy, somewhat exaggerated details. They all laughed. I forced myself to laugh with them, but I was uncomfortable being the brunt of the joke—especially sitting right across from the victim herself. Roshayne looked just as uncomfortable.

"I guess that's one way to meet girls," Scott laughed.

"Not if you ever want to talk to them again," Paul joked, smiling. He shot a quick glance at Roshayne and me.

As the topic ran its course, the brunette leaned forward, resting her chin in her hands and looking me dead in the eye. "So, what's your name, handsome?" she asked in a husky voice.

"Oh, my goodness gracious," squeaked Neil in a high falsetto. "Where ARE my manners?" He jumped to his feet. Reverting to his deepest bass, he announced, "Girls, this here is Bart. He's a real live California beach bum."

"That's sure a nice tan you've got there," observed the blonde.

"Bart, may I present the attractive miss Tamara," Neil said with a stiff half-bow in the direction of the brunette. "And this lovely lady," he said, indicating the blonde, "is Jill." He finished with a low bow, one hand on his stomach, and the other fluttering high over his head. Being in Jill's presence had transformed Neil into a real goofball. Jill loved it, though, and squealed with delight.

Jill asked Tamara about one of her classes, and soon all six were deep in conversation about their schedules, the football games, people they hadn't seen all summer, and all the other exciting new high school stuff. I just sat back and observed. Every few minutes, Roshayne looked over at me with her huge brown eyes and gave me the very faintest of Mona Lisa smiles.

So, am I finally forgiven? Is there a chance that she might even like me a little?

Later, Paul and Scott and I took turns dancing with Tamara and Roshayne during some of the fast dances. Roshayne was careful not to let me touch her. She wouldn't even let me lead her by the hand to the dance floor. Slow dances were out, of course—except for Neil and Jill, who were stuck to each other like glue.

After an hour or so of dancing, Scott suggested, "Let's get out of here. I'm tired of this place."

Paul piped in, "Hey, what say we go to the Freeze for some ice cream?"

"How are we going to get there?" asked Tamara. "Fly?"

Neil stood up and treated us to another bow. "Never fear. Neil is here."

Our appointed chauffeur was about to carry his first fare. We spilled out into the parking lot and were shown the way to the oldest, most decrepit looking excuse for a vehicle that I had ever laid eyes on.

"It's a pile of rust," I objected.

"Well, it runs," Neil said proudly. "And that's all that counts. Get in." We crammed ourselves in as best we could. Jill sat by Neil in the front, with Scott riding shotgun. Paul and I performed our gentlemanly duties by opening the back doors for Roshayne and Tamara. I was disappointed when Roshayne opted for Paul's side. *She's just playing hard to get,* I rationalized.

The girls squeezed into the middle, and we had to hold our breath to get the doors closed. I had to bang my door hard three times before it stayed shut.

"We've been meaning to fix that door," Neil told me. "We just never seem to get around to it. Be careful it doesn't open up on you."

"Are you sure this thing will get us there and back?" I asked.

"Sure," he said. "My brothers have been driving this little beauty for years."

That's what I was afraid of, I said to myself.

I detected the faint odor of a sweet, flowery perfume coming from one of the girls in the car—I wasn't sure which. I smiled to myself. *This is the life. Good friends. Beautiful women. Fast car. What more could a guy want? Maybe Utah's not so bad, after all.*

Suddenly, I felt goose bumps on my arms, as though a blast of cold air had blown through the car. I knew it hadn't, since all the doors and windows were closed, and we weren't moving yet. It gave me a creepy feeling. *Something's wrong here,* I thought.

But everything around me appeared to be perfectly normal. As quickly as it came, the feeling passed. I shrugged it off.

The car's engine turned over forever and ever before it finally coughed and kicked in. Surprisingly, it sounded smooth and quiet once it got going. Neil popped the clutch, giving us all a good whiplash, and we jerked our way out of the parking lot. With Jill sitting practically on top of Neil, he was more than a little distracted. We ran two stop signs going through town and almost missed the last turn. With tires screeching, Neil braked hard and yanked on the wheel. We were all thrown around on top of each other. The girls squealed and the guys laughed. I had never been quite that close to a pretty girl before, and having Tamara falling all over me was really something. Neil made some zigzag swerves to repeat the effect as we went down the highway. I just prayed that there weren't any cops in the neighborhood, and was grateful when we finally pulled into the parking lot in one piece.

The Freeze was a very popular, old fashioned, walk-up style hamburger joint, without an inside eating area. After our long wait in line, we took our banana splits and sundaes and went back to the car. I let Roshayne get plenty ahead of me and then climbed in beside her.

"So, now where?" Neil asked.

"Let's take a spin up the canyon," Tamara suggested. "All in favor?"

"Sure." "Okay." "Why not?"

"So, where do you live, Mr. Bart?" asked Tamara as we pulled out on the highway. Her interest in me was accelerating rapidly, which bothered me a little. I should have been flattered, but my own interests were decidedly elsewhere at the moment.

"They bought the Tanner place," Paul answered for me.

"The Tanners sold their farm?" asked Roshayne.

"Not the whole farm. Just the house. They built a new one a little ways down the road."

I elaborated, "They built a tall white fence around the sides and back of our yard, so we wouldn't have access to the horse barns and corrals and stuff. They still run the farm."

"We never did learn your last name," Tamara pushed on.

"I don't think I heard yours, either, Miss Tamara," I countered. *Two can play this game.*

"Edmonds," she responded. She raised her eyebrows at me expectantly.

"And yours, Miss Jill?" I asked to the front seat. Jill was caught totally off guard. Her interests were obviously elsewhere, too.

"Oh . . . uh . . . Jill," she said. "I mean Frampton. Jill Frampton."

"Elderberry."

"Huh?" asked Tamara.

"My last name is Elderberry. E-L-D-E-R-B-E-R-R-Y."

"You're kidding," Paul cut in, feigning surprise. He'd already heard my name a dozen times in school. "Elderberry? You sure it's not Blackberry or Blueberry?" he asked smiling. "Or maybe Gooseberry?" He laughed. "What's your mom's maiden name, Bart? Pie?" He laughed again. "Get it? Elderberry Pie?" He laughed hysterically and slapped his thighs. "Or maybe it's Pudding."

"Oh, yeah? So what about you?" Neil said, looking in the mirror at Paul. "When you get old, and they make you the bishop, you'll be Bishop Bishop." Everyone laughed. It felt good to feel accepted—to be part of the gang. It brought a little lump to my throat.

The gaiety escalated as everyone tried to one-up the joke before. Soon we were laughing so hard, and our eyes were watering so much, we could hardly see. Eventually it didn't matter if someone told a joke or not. We laughed at anything and everything, falling all over each other in the car. By the time we reached the mouth of the canyon, my side hurt from laughing so hard.

Suddenly, I was hit again with the same blast of cold air as before. I shivered involuntarily and had the distinct impression that we should turn around and go straight home.

Roshayne felt me shaking and asked, "Are you okay? You look like you're freezing to death."

"I just got a really creepy feeling," I said.

"You're just getting chilled from the ice cream," she responded. "You'll warm back up in a minute or two."

"I suppose," I answered evasively.

The feeling persisted. I couldn't shake it off. I kept imagining that I heard a voice somewhere off in the distance . . . calling my name . . . trying to get my attention.

If only I had listened.

CHAPTER 5

- *The Canyon* -

I recognized immediately where we were going. Dad had brought the family up the canyon the previous Sunday afternoon right after church while dinner was in the oven. It was really pretty in the daytime. The hillsides were covered with trees that grew right up to the edge of the road. The leaves were turning every color imaginable. We had to put our faces right up against the windows in order to see the tops of the mountains rising above us. Occasionally we caught a glimpse of a stream winding through the trees. Charlene and Cynthia squealed with delight whenever a squirrel or chipmunk ran across the road.

Having mountains so close was a new experience for us. Dad told us stories about all the beautiful lakes and meadows that were farther on up, and he promised us camping and fishing trips the next summer.

At night, however, the canyon was nothing at all like I remembered. It was a nightmare. As we wound up and around the endless turns and switchbacks, the road seemed twice as narrow as before. With only the smallest sliver of a moon visible, the trees were barely discernible as black and gray shadows along the road. For someone who had spent most of his life on the beach, it was an unnerving and harrowing experience at best. I started to feel a little carsick.

As we drove farther and farther up the winding canyon road, the others carried on as though nothing in the world was wrong.

"So what did you think of the football game yesterday?" Scott asked. The boys kicked that around for a bit.

"Did you see that dress Linda was wearing at the dance?" Roshayne interjected. "Wasn't it just horrible?" Tamara and Jill jumped in, and the girls took over.

"Sure is pitch black out here tonight," I said nervously during a break in the conversation. "I can hardly see the edge of the road."

"Yeah, and these bozos keep coming at me with their bright lights on," Neil complained as he squinted against another pair of oncoming headlights.

"It's almost eleven-thirty," Tamara spoke up. "Maybe we should be heading back down to the church."

The others agreed. After another couple of miles, Neil found a wide spot in the road and turned around. Two or three minutes later, we heard a noisy pickup truck coming up on our tail. He didn't approve of our slow descent, and began honking his horn and flashing his bright lights at us.

"Idiot!" Neil muttered under his breath. He reached up and twisted the mirror down to keep the light out of his eyes.

"What does he think this is?" Scott asked. "The Indy 500?"

The driver of the truck continued his steady honking and maneuvered to within a few feet of our rear bumper. We all watched anxiously over our shoulders.

"Why doesn't he just go around?" asked Tamara.

"The road's too narrow and winding for that," answered Neil.

"Then pull over and let him go by," Roshayne suggested.

"I can't find any place wide enough."

Scott started digging around and located his seat belt, which he promptly fastened. None of us had bothered with them previously. It would have appeared sissy. We could hear the truck's engine revving loudly as the driver closed the gap to within inches. Neil tapped on the brakes to make the brake lights come on, and the truck backed off a little. He soon guessed our game and closed in again. Neil applied a little pressure to the gas pedal to avoid being bumped from behind. The truck backed off again as we approached a turn, which we rounded a little faster than was comfortable.

"Slow down a little," Jill urged. "You're starting to scare me."

"I'm just trying to stay a little ahead of them," Neil explained.

On the next straightaway, the truck came up again and succeeded in bumping our car from behind, giving us a minor whiplash effect and a major scare. Neil accelerated again. Another curve came up quickly, and the tires squealed as we leaned into the turn.

Jill started to panic. "Neil, please!" she pleaded. "Slow down!"

By then, the truck was several yards behind us and appeared to be having just as much difficulty taking the corners as we were. But he continued honking and flashing his lights to annoy us. The next turn was a curve to the right, and we went halfway out into the left lane trying to recover from the turn. We would surely have hit any oncoming traffic, had there been any.

"He's backed off," I finally said with relief, watching intently over my shoulder. "Slow down a little."

After several seconds, it still didn't seem like we were slowing down at all. Paul grabbed Neil's shoulder and shook it. "Come on, Neil. Slow down. This isn't funny."

"I'm trying to!" he yelled back.

"What's wrong?" I asked, immediately alarmed. I could feel a cold chill coming over me again.

"The brakes are going soft! I can't get them to grab!"

"What!" screamed Jill.

"Omagosh!" cried Tamara.

My blood ran cold. "Pump 'em—!"

"I'm pumping! I'm pumping!" he roared. "They're gone! I can't stop!"

"We're going to die!" Tamara screamed.

We took the next left curve at breathtaking speed, using every inch we could of the left lane. At the end of the turn, it was all Neil could do to keep from running off the road into the mountain wall on the right.

"Use the gears!" yelled Scott. "Shift down! Shift down!"

Neil grabbed the gearshift on the steering column and tried to shift down. There was a terrible grinding sound. He let it off and tried again.

"It's no good!" he yelled. "We're going too fast! I can't get it into any gear now!"

"How far to town?" I demanded.

"About five miles! We'll never make it!"

Pandemonium set in. Everyone started yelling at once. Tamara screamed loudly. I gripped the handhold on the door to keep from being thrown around.

Another right curve came up all too quickly, and Neil swerved into the left lane to get a wider start. The tires squealed again as he fought to keep the car on the asphalt. Roshayne and Tamara both tumbled on top of Paul. I was afraid that if the tires slipped off into the gravel shoulder, we might never get back on the road again.

No one was watching the truck anymore. All eyes were fixed on the road ahead. Our speed was steadily increasing, making the turns more and more unmanageable. Another left turn came. Neil started the turn on the far right, then cut quickly across to the extreme edge of the left lane to get every possible advantage out of the turn. The curve was sharp, and all four tires squealed loudly in protest. We ended up clear over to the right side again before the end of the curve. That time, the right tires left the pavement and the soft shoulder sucked us over into the side of the mountain. The right mirror and door handles were stripped away as we broadsided a couple of trees. Both right windows shattered in a shower of flying glass. Neil finally bounced us back onto the road—just in time for the next left turn. It was even harder than the previous one, and we were all thrown roughly against the right side of the car. The left tires lifted off the pavement.

When we came straight again, I started groping around my seat, trying to find my seat belt. *Doesn't this piece of junk have any seat belts?* I cursed under my breath. *Stupid old car!*

There was a moment of relief as we barreled down a short straightaway, then we came up on two tortuous hairpin turns. The first one was to the left, and we took it with the back wheels skidding and the rear end fishtailing. As we came back straight, we could hear gravel flying under the floorboards as the rear left wheel slipped briefly off the road, just inches from the edge. We were in the center of the road when we started into the right turn. Neil yanked the wheel hard to the right in a desperate attempt to make the corner.

We were going too fast, and the turn was too sharp. The right side of the car lifted a full foot off the ground and started into a roll. Without thinking, Neil instinctively corrected by bringing the wheel left, and the right wheels came slamming back down on the pavement.

We were airborne a split second later.

I was momentarily stunned by the sudden quiet. All we could see were the stars and the wide-open sky through the front windshield. For a brief instant, it felt as though we were hanging suspended and motionless in midair. Then the stars were blocked out by treetops as the front end started coming down. We all screamed in unison at the tops of our lungs.

The front left wheel had been the first to leave the road and was the first to make contact again with the rock-strewn incline. The car hit hard at a steep angle, cutting our screams off abruptly as we were thrown violently forward. The buoyancy of the left tire caused the front end to leap back into the air again, bringing the right rear slamming down against the hillside. Everyone, except Scott, was thrown against the ceiling. Then the rear end bounced up again and threw us all back down into the seats. Roshayne slumped to the floor in a heap at my feet. The whole car fell pointing nose down, skimming over a boulder the size of a washing machine. The transmission and rear axle were ripped away, as well as the gas tank. The rest of the mangled car continued to careen wildly down the hill.

The old rusted latch and hinges of that stubborn right rear door had taken all the abuse they were going to take. The door snapped open and swung violently forward, then was torn completely free and cartwheeled down a ravine. In spite of having been tossed around like a rag doll in a clothes dryer, I was still clutching the handle of that door in a death grip. When it opened, I was abruptly pulled up and propelled out through the open doorway like a pilot ejecting from a jet—straight up twenty or thirty feet into the air.

CHAPTER 6

- Near Death -

As I was thrown from the car, I was struck with an overwhelming panic and began clawing at the air with my arms and legs—screaming for all I was worth.

I don't want to die! my mind raced. *I DON'T WANT TO DIE!!*

As I came to the top of the arch, some thirty feet in the air, I found myself facing down, with arms and legs outstretched. I knew with a certainty that I was about to be dashed to pieces on the rocks below. I knew there was no escape. No chance. No options.

"NOOOOOOO!!" I screamed out. I closed my eyes tight. My limbs continued their frantic search for something, anything, that would break my fall. There was nothing but air.

"NOOOOOOOO!!" I continued screaming and screaming. I felt the rush of wind in my face as I started the downward plunge.

"NOOOOoooooo . . ."

And then there was nothing.

The scream died. The wind in my face stopped. The smashing, crushing force of body against rocks did not come.

I opened my eyes.

This can't be! I was suspended in the air, ten or fifteen feet above the ground—just hanging there.

Time has stopped, I reasoned. *My mind is rushing at such high speed, it looks like time has slowed down. That must be it. Any second now the fall will be over, and I'll be . . .*

Dead? So, this is it, I thought matter-of-factly. *I'm dead. It didn't even hurt.*

The ground started to settle away from me, and I realized that I was floating upwards. I felt as light as a fluff of feather. There was no sensation of rising, falling, or moving at all. I felt . . . free, as though heavy chains had been removed.

Strangely, I felt ALIVE! More alive than I had ever felt before.

As I continued to rise, ever so slowly, I became more aware of my surroundings. Even though it was pitch dark—and I KNEW it was pitch dark—I could see everything around me in great detail. Every limb and stone and blade of grass. The ground below me was not as rocky and rough as I had feared. It was covered with thick underbrush and small trees. As I looked into the brush, I caught sight of someone's arm and head protruding from under a clump of scrub oak.

That's Bartholomew Elderberry, I observed, without any emotion whatsoever. I knew Bartholomew Elderberry was me, but the body I was looking at no longer held any interest for me. Strange.

I'm done with that body now, I reasoned. *I don't need it anymore.*

I became aware of crystal clear sounds all around me, as though I was in the middle of a surround-sound system. I heard the leaves and limbs below me still rustling as they settled back into their original positions. I heard the sounds of metal against rock, branches snapping, and boulders tumbling. I heard people screaming, glass breaking, and metal twisting.

I also heard other sounds, equally sharp, that didn't make any sense—like a telephone ringing and a piano playing somewhere far away. I heard a dog barking and people laughing. I tried to shut them out and ignore them, but they were still there in the background—thousands and millions of individual sounds coming from everywhere, blending together into one beautiful symphony of its own.

I turned over and looked up into the sky. The stars seemed larger and brighter than I had ever seen. Almost blinding. They stretched endlessly in all directions. I knew instinctively that I could go to any of them, if I wanted. I could go ANYWHERE I wanted. I was free!

I started to rise more rapidly in the dark, open sky. Up and up toward the canopy of lights. The mountain peaks fell away below me. The twinkling lights of the town became visible at the bottom of the canyon and gradually grew closer and closer together. Then lights from neighboring towns joined in, and eventually all melded together into a small cluster. I continued to rise, higher and higher.

When I was too high to see the lights anymore, I turned my attention to the horizons. Toward the east it was very dark, but to the west I could see leftover light from the recent sunset, silhouetting the curvature of the earth's surface. At the edge, it was a beautiful dark blue and green. The earth appeared so perfect, all spread out in front of me like that. Higher still I rose, like a missile aiming for the moon.

I'm higher than any bird has ever flown, I thought. *Only the astronauts have ever seen the earth like this . . . and God,* I realized. *This is the way God sees the earth. No countries. No boundaries. Just endless, beautiful perfection.*

Thinking of God, I remembered, *There's supposed to be a light or angels or something coming to get me.* I directed my eyes to the sky again, searching, but seeing nothing that did not belong there. I stopped moving, perplexed. Something was not right. I had no idea where I was supposed to be going. I had always assumed someone would be there to greet me, like Peter at the Pearly Gates.

Maybe I'm being given a chance to say goodbye first. I thought about Mom and Dad, and my brothers and sisters—

No sooner did that thought come to mind than I was moving again at lightning speed, back down toward the surface of the earth. In the blink of an eye, I found myself hovering over our front porch. I was astonished at the speed at which I had traveled, and the total absence of motion.

The lights were on in the living room, and I had an intense desire to see my parents one last time. I moved toward the front door and reached for the knob. My hand and arm went right through as though it wasn't there at all, and I was suddenly standing in the air inside the entryway. My mother was sitting in her rocking chair, reading a magazine. She looked so peaceful.

"Mom!" I called out. *"Mom, I'm here! I came back to say goodbye!"* Somehow, I had assumed that she would hear me and see me. She didn't move.

She doesn't know, I realized. *She doesn't know I'm dead. She's going to be sad.* I moved over to her side, trying to touch her shoulder.

"Don't be sad, Mom. I'm still alive. I feel wonderful!"

She smiled a little at something she was reading, and I saw, for the first time in my life, what a beautiful lady she was.

I moved down the hall toward my father's den and found him sitting at his desk. He was poring over a pile of papers scattered across the entire surface.

"You're a good father, Dad," I said, even though I knew he couldn't hear me. *"I love you."*

The very words surprised me. I hadn't said those words to my parents for a long, long time. I wished I had said them more often. I watched him work for a minute, then continued up the stairs to each of the girls' bedrooms. They were both sound asleep and looked so sweet and peaceful.

"I'll miss you both," I said softly. Next I moved to Darin's room. *"I'm sorry I've always been so mean to you. I guess you get to be the oldest now."*

I wanted to see Chris again, but I didn't know where he was, except that he was somewhere in California. I moved back out through the front door, reaching again to turn the knob.

I can't touch things, I reminded myself. *I'm a spirit now.*

Out in the front yard, I gazed into heaven and called out, *"I'm ready now."*

Unexpectedly, in the midst of the millions of sounds in the background, I heard my name.

"BAAAAART!!" It was a girl's voice—loud, prolonged, and desperate.

It's Roshayne!

I looked in the direction of the canyon from where the voice originated, and the recollection of the events that had just transpired came flooding back to me. Without any conscious effort on my part, I found myself moving back to the mountains. Back to the site of the accident—to the site of my death.

In another instant, I was hovering over the crumpled remains of Neil's car. Paramedics were bending over two people by the wreck, and Search and Rescue workers were slowly hoisting a stretcher up the mountainside. Dozens of emergency vehicles lined the road, with red and blue lights flashing everywhere.

I became aware of other people moving around among the trees along the hillside. They had flashlights and seemed to be looking for something.

They're looking for me! They're looking for my body!

Then, an astonishing thing happened. I heard—actually I FELT a loud snap and was pulled uncontrollably back to my body. With a violent jerk, I was yanked back inside. The feelings of airiness disappeared. I felt heavy again. I felt trapped and tied down. The symphony of sound died. I opened my eyes and was smothered by the intense, thick blackness, causing a wave of claustrophobia to come over me. I heard some voices nearby and the sounds of twigs and leaves crunching. A bright light appeared directly over my head, causing me to squint and turn aside.

Then I felt the pain—intense, unbearable pain coming from my arms and legs, my back, and everywhere, it seemed. I heard a garbled, throaty cry coming from somewhere, and realized it was my own.

"We found him! We found him!" a voice yelled from behind the light. "He's alive!"

It was already into the wee hours of the morning by the time Roshayne and I were loaded into the last two ambulances. Jill had been rushed down in the first one. Scott, Paul, Tamara, and Neil had been taken down not far ahead of us. As they lifted Roshayne into the ambulance, I saw that she was completely immobilized on a stretcher, the same as I was, and I wondered briefly about everyone else's condition.

At last we were making our way down the canyon. I soon forgot about the others, and was only vaguely aware of the I.V. being started in my arm. I was too busy fighting my own pain, and trying to sort things out at the same time. I was still confused about how and why I was back in my body and not dead. It had seemed so final and right . . . and wonderful. Being alive was disappointing.

Looking up at the ceiling of the ambulance brought back memories that had been suppressed for a long time. I thought back to another time when I had been lying on a similar stretcher. *Something weird had happened,* I thought. But my mind became groggy and out of focus. *What was it?* I closed my eyes to concentrate. *They had me strapped down to the stretcher,* I remembered vaguely, *and I wanted to get up. Then . . . then . . .* I couldn't concentrate. The thoughts kept slipping away. *I was . . . floating . . .* Everything around me started to spin, and I felt groggier than ever. *. . . the roof . . .* My eyes fell shut, and my mind turned to mush. I couldn't stop it.

When I awoke, I was in a bed in a hospital room. Mom was standing over me, holding my hand, her cheeks stained with tears. Dad was right behind her with his arm around her waist.

"Thank the Lord you're all right," Mom said, smiling. "Thank the Lord."

A nurse came up along the left side of the bed and asked me how I was feeling.

"I'm not sure," I answered truthfully.

"You're a very lucky boy, Bartholomew," she said. "Nothing short of a miracle."

"What happened?" I asked, still trying to clear the cobwebs.

"You were in an accident. Do you remember the accident?"

"Yeah, I think so." What I remembered clearly was floating around in the stars, but I didn't tell her that.

"The paramedics said you were thrown from the car and landed in some big, thorny bushes. Not a single bone broken. Your clothes were in shreds, though, and you have cuts and bruises all over the place. You're going to feel pretty sore for a while."

"I feel like I just got run over by a truck," I mumbled.

I noticed that there was light coming in through the window. "What time is it?" I asked. "How long have I been here?"

"It's about two o'clock," Mom answered. "Your dad just came back from church. I've been here with you all night and all morning." She looked as if she hadn't slept a wink for days. So much different than how I had seen her in the living room the night before.

Did I really see her there? Or was it a dream?

"Everybody's praying for you," Dad said. "All seven of you."

I heard some voices in the hall as Scott and Roshayne and their parents came through the door and up to the bedside. Roshayne had a big bandage on her forehead and a few others on her arms. She also appeared to be limping a little.

"How you doing, beach bum?" joked Scott.

"Hi, Bart," Roshayne said.

"Hi. Are you guys okay?" I asked. "Last night you were both on stretchers."

"Just cuts and bruises," she said, pointing to the bandages on her arms. "I have about a dozen more of these that you can't see—and seventeen stitches." She gave a little choked laugh, then sniffled.

The nurse added, "You have a few dozen yourself, Bart."

"How about you?" I asked Scott.

"I had the wind knocked out of me pretty good, but I'm okay."

"What about the other guys?" I asked. Roshayne and Scott exchanged glances.

"Paul has his right leg in a brace right now," explained Scott. "It broke just above the ankle. The doctor said it was a clean break and should heal okay. They have to do some surgery on it later today, so he'll probably be here a day or two."

"Tammy has her right arm in a cast," added Roshayne. "She's pretty shook up."

"What about Neil?" I asked.

"He's going to be here for a while," Scott answered. "He broke some ribs and punctured a lung, among other things. He's down the hall just a couple of doors from here."

"We're going to go see him in a few minutes," Roshayne said.

"And Jill?"

They both looked nervously at the floor.

"Jill . . ." Roshayne began, fighting her emotions. "Jill . . ." she tried again.

Mom came to her rescue. "Jill is still unconscious, Bart," she said softly. "She was in the emergency room all morning. They have her in the intensive care unit now, and her condition is very critical." She paused. "It doesn't look good, Bart."

The nurse spoke up to change the subject. "Dr. Pearson will be here to see you a little later, when he makes his rounds. If he thinks you're doing okay, he could let you go home today."

"We brought you some more clothes," Dad said cheerfully, holding up a bag for me to see.

"Let's let Bart get a little more rest before he leaves," the nurse suggested as she began ushering everyone toward the door.

"We're going to go make a quick phone call," Dad said as they moved to follow, "and let the kids know you're all right. We'll be right back."

"Mom? Dad?" I called after them.

They stopped and turned.

"What is it, son?"

I looked them each in the eye for a long moment as a big lump formed in my throat.

"I love you, Dad. I love you, Mom," I choked out, my lip quivering.

Mom erupted in tears. "Oh, Bart." She rushed back and kissed me gently on the cheek. "We love you, too, honey."

Even Dad was looking misty-eyed when they left.

CHAPTER 7

- NDEs & OBEs -

The nurse was right. I hurt like crazy for a while. I came home later Sunday night and stayed home from school for three days. At first, it was all I could do to get up and go to the bathroom, but by Wednesday evening I was wandering around the house bored out of my gourd, so Mom decided it was time for me to go back to school.

The minute I walked through the doors, I gained celebrity status. News of the accident had spread like wildfire, and everybody I ran into wanted to hear the whole thing firsthand. Each of my classes that day began with my ten-minute synopsis, which I got plenty tired of by last period.

Neil was still in the hospital. Jill continued unconscious and was officially listed as comatose. They had stitched up her scalp and repaired her face as best they could, and both wrists were in casts. The doctors were not optimistic that she would wake up very soon.

Scott never missed a day, and all of our teachers used him as the shining example of what seat belts were all about.

I was miles behind in all my classes, of course, and was buried up to my chin in books and homework through the rest of the week and into the weekend.

The next Monday morning, I caught Paul's arm as we got off the bus at school. "I need to talk to you," I said.

"You'll have to talk fast," Paul replied impatiently. "My first class is physics, and it's a long walk from here on one leg."

"I didn't mean now. It'll take a few minutes."

"Okay," he said. "When?"

"I was thinking maybe during study hall. How about it?"

"Sure."

"Okay. Meet me in the hall outside the auditorium."

I fidgeted my way through every class waiting for study hall, and told myself a hundred times I was making a big mistake telling anybody.

Finally it was time. On my way to meet Paul, I made a last-minute detour to the library. Roshayne was just walking in the door with an armload of books.

"Rosh," I called out, just loud enough for her to hear.

"Hi, Bart," she said, smiling. "How are you feeling?"

"Better," I said quickly. "Listen, I was just going to meet Paul. I have some things I want to tell you both." She looked hesitant. "It's about the accident," I added.

"What ABOUT the accident?" she asked, suddenly concerned.

"Something strange happened to me that I haven't told anybody about. I wanted you and Paul to be the first."

"What do you mean, 'something strange'?" she asked, raising her eyebrows.

"Come on, and I'll tell you," I grabbed her gently by the arm and headed her down the hall. She looked at me real puzzled and resisted my nudges.

"Please, Rosh. It's really important," I pleaded.

"Okay," she finally agreed, seeing how serious I was.

I headed down the hall at a brisk walk.

"But it better be short," she said, trying to catch up. "I've got some pre-calc that I need to work on."

Paul was waiting dutifully in the hallway, leaning on his crutches. He raised his eyebrows when he saw Roshayne with me, but didn't say anything. I unlocked the door and led them in.

"So, what's all this about?" asked Paul as we settled into the folding seats. I waited for the doors to swing shut and my eyes to adjust to the semi-darkness. They both watched me intently, waiting.

"Something happened to me at the accident," I said, almost in a whisper. "Something very, very weird." I paused again, not sure how to start.

"What?" Roshayne asked impatiently.

"I'm getting to it," I said. "I've spent the last eight days trying to figure out how to tell you this. Or whether I should tell you at all."

"I'm sorry, Bart," she said. "You're just acting a little strange, that's all."

"I want you both to promise me that you won't laugh at me, or tell me I'm crazy. Promise?"

"Promise," they said.

I took a deep breath. "When the car went over the hill and I was thrown out, I separated from my body and was left floating in the air." I glanced at each of them quickly to see their reactions. Both were staring blankly, as though waiting for me to say "Just kidding." "I'm not kidding, you guys. I could see my body lying there in the bushes, just like it was somebody else." Paul's mouth dropped open. Roshayne's eyes were hard. I looked back and forth, waiting for them to say something. "I knew it," I said, folding my arms and sitting back, disgusted. "I should never have said anything. I knew you wouldn't believe me."

When I looked up at Paul again, he was smiling broadly.

"Bart," he said excitedly, "are you saying you had an NDE? A real live NDE?"

"A what?" Roshayne and I both asked.

"An NDE," he said, as though it was something every kindergarten kid should know. "You know. A Near Death Experience."

Roshayne cut in, "If flying off a cliff at fifty miles an hour isn't a near death experience, I don't know what is. We ALL just about died, you know."

"No, you don't understand," he explained. "A Near Death Experience is when your spirit leaves your body for a while, then comes back in. Some people call them OBEs—Out of Body Experiences. Lots of people have had them—you'd be surprised. Usually it happens as part of an accident, just like ours." He looked at me again, getting more excited by the minute. "What happened? Tell us what happened."

Roshayne looked at Paul, then back at me. "Yeah, tell us, Bart. This REALLY better be good."

So I told them. I told them about floating in the air, and about flying out into space. I told them about rushing back down to my home and seeing my family. I told them about being invisible and passing through the front door. And finally about hearing Roshayne's voice and rushing back to the mountain.

" . . . and there I was. Back in my body and being carried up the hill on a stretcher." There was a profound silence when I finished.

"What did it feel like?" Paul asked, intrigued.

"Well, like I was . . . I don't know . . . a puff of smoke . . . or a mist. I knew I was made of something, but it was kind of . . . airy, I guess."

"Bart Elderberry," Roshayne interrupted, disgusted. "You have just about the BIGGEST imagination of anybody I have ever met. I've never heard ANYTHING like it. I can't believe you hauled me in here to listen to this . . . this—"

"You think I made this up?" I asked. It never occurred to me that they would call me a liar. "Are you calling me a liar?"

Paul cut in. "Rosh, things like this happen. There are a dozen books written about people you have had NDEs like this. Why not Bart? I, for one, believe every word he said. I think it's neat."

"Those books are about psychos and weirdoes," Roshayne said. Realizing she was outnumbered, she backed down a little. "Okay. So let's ASSUME this happened. Not that I believe it, of course. How would it happen? I mean . . . why?" She looked back at me. "You've got to admit, this is pretty off the wall."

"Rosh, I don't know why. And I certainly don't know how. All I know is that it happened."

"You probably just dreamed it. Maybe you hit your head and hallucinated or something."

"I expected you to say that," I replied. "I don't know how to convince you, but I know—I absolutely, positively, one hundred percent KNOW that I was not dreaming. I was conscious the whole time. And I can prove it."

"How?" she demanded.

"I can tell you things about the wreck that I wouldn't have been able to know any other way." I proceeded, "When I went back to the mountains, you were lying on the ground with a paramedic leaning over you, and you were yelling my name. Scott was just a few feet away."

"Scott could have told you that," she defended.

"Okay. I also looked down on the car from overhead. It was upside down by an embankment and a big tree. The back wheels were missing. The Search and Rescue guys were carrying a stretcher up the hill, and there were two more by the car, lined up end to end. Neil was on the front one and Paul was on the back one."

"That's right," Paul defended. "Jill went first, 'cause she was such a mess. Tammy and Scott and Roshayne were taken up later, when more stretchers got there."

"You still could have learned all that from somebody," Roshayne fought back.

I thought some more. "I know exactly what my mother was reading that night. And my dad was balancing his checkbook."

"You could have already asked them," she countered.

"I don't know what else to say, Rosh," I conceded, "except that it's true."

"Well, I don't believe it," she said, standing up. "I've got some studying to do. You two can just sit here and make up your stupid sci-fi stories."

"But—"

She stormed out through the doors.

"Come on," Paul said, gathering up his crutches. "We're going to be late for seminary."

I spent the better part of the next two weeks reading everything I could get my hands on that even remotely resembled NDEs and OBEs. Paul was right. There were written accounts of hundreds of people from all over the country and all around the world—even little kids.

We had just been given an assignment in English to write a research paper, so I decided to do mine on Near Death Experiences. My parents were a little surprised at how quickly I left the dinner table every night to study. I even turned down dessert once because I was right in the middle of an exciting book and couldn't wait to get back. Mom made some joke about me being sick and came over to feel my forehead. In school, it became very difficult to concentrate on my other classes.

Paul and I met regularly in our secret spot in the auditorium and discussed my findings as I went. He was excited and eager to hear my reports. I invited Roshayne to come and listen. At first she refused, but eventually her curiosity got the better of her and she came along, "just to listen," she said.

One time we met, I told them, "You know, I've been thinking."

"Uh-oh, that's dangerous," Roshayne joked.

"Very funny. No, seriously. Something you said the other day about all this being a dream. You remember?"

"Yeah."

"Well, it reminded me of a dream I had in third grade. I used to think about it a lot, but I haven't for a while. Now, the more I think about it, the more I'm convinced that I've done this before."

"You mean you had another NDE before?" Paul asked surprised. "When? What happened?"

"Well, I was in the hospital having my appendix taken out. I remember it hurt a lot afterwards, and I cried a lot, so they gave me a shot to take the pain away. It worked for a while, and I slept a little. Then the pain started coming back—real bad. I couldn't stand it. I tried to call the nurse, but she didn't hear."

"Why didn't you just push the button?" asked Roshayne.

"I didn't know there was any button. I was only nine. Anyway, I felt this really terrible pain, and I remember thinking to myself, 'I don't want any more pain. Why can't I just die? I'd rather die.' Then I had this dream—at least I always thought it was a dream."

"About what?"

"I dreamed I had died and was floating around on the ceiling above the bed—like a balloon. I watched my body for a little while, lying there dead. Then the nurse came in and put a needle in the I.V. She thought I was just sleeping and didn't pay any attention. I thought it was funny that she didn't see me on the ceiling. After she left, I got thinking, 'That's probably more pain medicine she put in there, so it probably doesn't hurt anymore.' I decided that I didn't want to die after all, and I went back into my body. Just like that. And I was right. It DIDN'T hurt anymore."

"Wow," Paul said.

"I told the nurse about it the next time she came in, you know."

"What did she say?"

"She said it was not unusual to have these weird kinds of visions when you're all drugged up on painkillers. That's what she called them. Visions. So, I believed her. She was a nurse, after all. And an adult. What did I know?"

"How many people have you found in your books that have

had more than one NDE?" Paul asked.

"I don't remember. Only one or two that I can think of. I'll have to check."

The first Saturday in October, I was invited to Scott's birthday party. He had planned an afternoon of horseback riding up the canyon and had invited a couple of dozen guys and girls. At first I was a little leery, having never been on a horse before, but Paul talked me into it.

"You're in Utah now," he said. "It's about time you mounted up."

I was surprised to find out how many people had their own horses. Roshayne borrowed one from her uncle. I borrowed one from Paul. We packed up a picnic and planned to spend most of the day riding into the hills and back again. Neil was also invited, but he was still pretty sore from the accident, and since Jill was still in a coma, he wasn't much into fun and games anyway.

We met just south of the high school, with the horses arriving in trailers. Scott led the way, and the rest of us just let our horses follow him. We had a real good time talking and laughing. Every once in a while, when we found a big enough area, some of the guys would race their steeds, but I was afraid to try that. Paul was still in a walking cast, so he didn't race either.

We came upon the wreck quite suddenly, and it took me totally by surprise. In fact, it took me a second to realize that it was OUR wreck. Some of the others joked about how nobody could have survived a crash like that.

"This reminds me of a joke," one girl said. "When I die, I want to go in my sleep, nice and peaceful, like my grandpa . . ." She paused.

"And . . . ?" someone prompted.

" . . . not screaming and hollering and scared to death, like the other four people in his car."

They all laughed. When they realized that the four of us were not amused, but were just staring at the wreck, they finally realized that we WERE the survivors.

"Oh, you guys!" she said, all embarrassed. "I'm sorry!"

Almost in unison, Scott, Paul, Roshayne, and I dismounted. It was a spooky feeling, seeing that car in broad daylight, so totally destroyed. We suddenly realized how lucky we really were. We could see the path where it had plowed its way down the hill, and the rear axle still sitting by itself farther up on the hill. We walked around and studied it for several minutes. There were more than a couple of silent prayers offered in thanksgiving.

While we were standing there, a strange feeling came over me. It was as if I was experiencing déjà vu or something. I realized that I had never seen the wreck in the flesh, yet I knew every detail perfectly. I tried to calculate the exact position from which I had viewed it the first time. I had been directly overhead, maybe fifty or sixty feet off the ground. I looked all around. There was nothing within hundreds of feet in any direction at that level—except thin air. I felt a wave of relief and satisfaction flood over me. Up until that moment, there had still been those nagging doubts. In spite of what I had told Roshayne, I had never really been so one hundred percent sure that I hadn't been dreaming. Suddenly, the proof was right in front of my eyes. I HAD been out of my body, fully conscious and fully aware. It was an awesome feeling.

As we were leaving, Roshayne stooped over and picked up a plastic banana split container near the car. She looked at me intently, remembering our ride up the canyon.

"It wasn't the ice cream that made you cold, was it?" she asked.

CHAPTER 8

- English -

School got really busy, and I had to spend more and more of my evenings doing homework—sometimes clear 'til midnight. As a result of all the late-night studying, I was really tired one particular Friday in school, and I had to concentrate hard to stay awake. In history, I kept dozing off and my head would jerk a little. I would look around real quick to see if anybody had noticed. Lucky for me, I was sitting in the back, so nobody seemed to care.

I wasn't so lucky in English. My desk was right in the front. It didn't take long before my eyelids started drooping again. I tried to sit up real straight with my arms folded, so I could stay alert. It didn't work. Twice my head dropped, and I jerked back awake. The girl to my right giggled, but the teacher didn't notice.

The third time, I lost it. I was staring high up on the wall with my head tipped back when my eyes started to close again. All of a sudden, I felt a strange tingling sensation go through my whole body. It went up and down from my head to my toes several times, then slowly died away.

Just as it quit, there was a loud THUD in front of me and a clatter of books and pencils sailing in all directions. I jerked opened my eyes and saw that the guy in front of me had collapsed face-down on his desk, his arms hanging limp over the sides. Everyone in the room was looking at him, wondering what had happened. The teacher came over to check him out. He shook the kid's shoulders, trying to wake him up, but he didn't move. He shook him again. I tried to remember who was sitting in front of me.

Then it struck me. *There isn't anybody sitting in front of me. I'M on the front row! That's supposed to be MY desk!* I whipped around to see who was sitting behind me and found myself nose to nose with some girl's face.

"Whoa!" I yelled, jerking back. She didn't even flinch. She acted as if she didn't even hear me. In fact, she was looking right through me as if I wasn't even there. At first I thought she must have been leaning way over her desk to see, but she was sitting straight up in her own chair. I looked down and discovered that I was waist deep, right smack dab in the middle of her desk!

"What's going on!" I yelled. I tried to grab the edges of the desk to push myself out, but my hands went right through the desktop. That brought me to my senses. It was the same as when I had tried the doorknob during the NDE. I spun back around, realizing finally that the kid out cold on the desk was—ME!

Holy cow! My body fell off!

I looked around the room and saw that everyone was watching intently as the teacher tried to rouse my body. The ones in the back were standing up for a better view, including Paul. No one was looking at me.

"What happened?" some of them were asking. "Is he dead?" I saw Paul start pushing his way to the front. "Is he all right?"

"I'm okay," I told them. No one heard.

What am I going to do? I can't let this happen right here in class! I've got to get back in!

SNAP! It was as if someone had grabbed my neck with one of those big hooks in the cartoons. I was jerked clean off my feet and back into my body with a resounding crack. I slowly opened my eyes and found myself looking at my out-of-focus desktop. My shoulders were being shaken roughly, so I sat up.

"I'm okay, already," I said as I pushed the teacher's arms away. "Quit shaking me."

He backed away, and several students gasped.

"I'm fine. I'm just tired, that's all."

"Honest to Pete, young man!" he said sternly. "Passing out on your desk is a little more than 'just tired,' if you ask me. You were down for the count. Are you on drugs?" He looked at me closer. "Your forehead is bleeding. You'd better go see the nurse."

I felt my forehead and discovered, along with a trickle of blood, a pretty respectable goose egg starting to form. I gathered up my things and stood up.

The teacher pointed at a couple of guys nearby. "You and you. Go with him and make sure he gets there in one piece."

"Sure," they said, jumping up.

Paul butted in, "Let me go with him, I'm—"

"Two is enough! He doesn't need the whole class. Now, everybody sit down and let's get back to work."

"But—"

"But nothing. Sit down!"

As soon as we left the room, I told the guys, "It's okay. Honest. I'll be fine."

"No way, José," one objected. "You don't think we're going back to class, do you? We're with you all the way."

"Yeah," insisted the other. "This could easily take us twenty or thirty minutes." They laughed. "So what DID happen in there?" he said seriously. "You took a pretty mean pop to the head."

"I had a pretty tough night last night. I guess I fell asleep. Good thing I wasn't driving, huh?"

The first guy stopped walking. "Hey, aren't you one of the guys who was in that accident a few weeks ago?" he asked.

"Yeah," agreed the second, studying me closely. "You're the one who got thrown out of that car, aren't you? I'll bet you're suffering some kind of delayed brain thing. You better go see a doc, man."

"I guess I better," I said agreeably. "Thanks, guys."

"Don't mention it."

They left me at the office and did their disappearing act. The school nurse put a big Band-Aid on my forehead and gave me some Tylenol for the pain.

By the time I had filled out all the paperwork, it was lunchtime. I tried to walk as inconspicuously as possible down the hall to my locker, but I felt like I had a neon sign flashing on my head, telling everybody, "Watch out! Here comes Mr. Klutz!" I made it to the lunchroom without anybody saying anything. I didn't see anybody from my English class, thank goodness. Gradually I realized that nobody really cared about me, or my stupid Band-Aid, and I was almost through eating before I felt comfortable enough to start analyzing what had happened.

I just had another NDE! Realization dawned. *But why? What made my body fall off?* I started getting worried. *Is this going to be like having epileptic seizures? Is my body just going to take a dive any old time it feels like it?* It was like the glue wouldn't stick or something. *And what about those vibrations?* I wondered. *I don't remember that happening at the accident.*

I wasn't hungry anymore.

Maybe I've got some kind of nervous disorder. I started to panic. *Those guys were right! I probably DO have brain damage!* I envisioned myself having all kinds of surgery and brain scans, and having my head cut open with knives and saws, and never going back to school. *Something must be seriously wrong with me. I'm not normal. This makes three times now that I've left my body.*

The thought of being hospitalized suddenly brought back the memory of my fifth-grade ambulance ride and all that weirdness. My mouth dropped open. "Holy Cow!" I blurted out, jumping up. I looked around at all the kids staring at me, and took my tray quickly to the counter. *This is the fourth time!* I thought in dismay. *THE FOURTH TIME!*

On the way to history, Paul found me.

"Hey, where were you? I looked all over." He saw the oversize Band-Aid on my forehead. "I thought you were a goner back there. What happened?"

"I was just tired, that's all," I lied again. "I fell asleep."

"Asleep, my foot! You fainted dead away!"

"I just fell asleep," I repeated irritably. "It's nothing to get all worked up about, okay?"

He backed off. "Okay, man. Whatever you say." He hurried off by himself.

I was worried sick all through supper. Mom, of course, had to know all about the Band-Aid and the goose egg. I gave her the same story as everyone else. I'm not sure she believed it, but she accepted it anyway.

I wondered if I should tell her what was going on. Maybe she would know something that I didn't—like aftereffects of my fifth-grade accident or something. What I needed desperately at that moment was for someone to tell me I was all right. After rehearsing a few variations in my head, I dismissed the idea. It was all just too crazy.

Later that night I lay awake in bed for some time, staring at the ceiling. After closing my eyes, I drifted in and out of that borderline state between asleep and awake, going over and over the events of the past few weeks. Just as I was about to slip away, I was startled by the same weird vibrations that I had felt in class. They made my whole body shake and quiver.

This is getting too strange, I thought. I didn't dare move a single muscle for fear things would start falling off again. I waited expectantly for several minutes, but nothing else happened. Finally I relaxed a little. *Maybe I'm just imagining things,* I thought, relieved. *I've got to hurry and get to sleep.*

I remembered that I needed to turn off the alarm clock so I could sleep in. Without opening my eyes, I reached over to the nightstand and felt around for the clock. My fingers found the edge of the table, then walked their way gingerly over some of the junk sitting there, like my wallet and wristwatch. Finding the clock radio, I felt around on top for the right button. Satisfied that I was in the right place, I pushed the button to the right. When I did, the button sank into the radio and disappeared.

Dumb thing. I need to get a new radio. I moved my finger back and tried it again. I felt the button against my fingertip and pushed slowly. Just when I knew it should be moving, it felt like it disappeared again.

Oh, come on! I opened my eyes and sat up in bed, then I reached for the clock to bring it over where I could see it. I felt it in my hand as I grabbed it, but when I closed my hand around it to pick it up, my fingers closed on themselves, right through the clock. I looked at the clock and at my hand in disbelief. Then I tried it again.

"OH, NO! NOT AGAIN!"

I turned around to look at the pillow and saw myself sleeping peacefully. It was a VERY weird feeling. Like looking in the mirror, only different. I looked backwards somehow. And the bump on my forehead looked tons bigger than it did in the mirror.

Curious, I thought about getting another view from a different angle. My spirit-self suddenly floated to the right and upwards. I didn't have to move my arms and legs at all.

Weird.

The memories of my flight into space came back to me, and I realized that everywhere I had gone that night had been a result of my thinking about the destination. I had looked at the stars, and I went there. When I thought about home, I was on the front porch. When I heard Roshayne calling, I was back at the mountain.

Down, I thought, and I floated down immediately. There wasn't even the slightest bit of delay. The thought "down" was barely half formed in my mind, and I was moving already.

Up, I commanded next. And there I was, floating against the ceiling.

Just like a balloon, I remembered. I could feel the ceiling bumping gently against my back. It felt kind of like trying to lie still on the bottom of a swimming pool. What really surprised me was that I could feel it at all. I looked down at the nightstand with my wallet and clock. *I felt all that stuff, just like I would have any other time.* I turned over, face up like a spider, and felt the ceiling with my fingertips. It was smooth and hard, just like a ceiling should be.

What if I want to go farther up?

The next part was really creepy. I went through the ceiling all right, but not fast, like I had gone through the front door. There was a moment or two of slight resistance, then I just sort of melted or sifted through. I felt the texture of the thin layer of paint as I passed through it, and then the chalky feel of the gypsum board. I felt the fluffiness of the insulation and the coarseness of the timbers and the shingles. It was all really strange. Before I knew it, I was hovering over our roof in the dark, struggling to comprehend what I had just done.

I still have a sense of touch, I marveled, *but only if I touch really slow and careful. If I go through things real fast, I won't feel anything.*

To prove that to myself, I clenched my fist and tried to punch a hole in the chimney to the side of me. As expected, my whole arm went right in without feeling a thing. I held it steady, buried up to my biceps in the brick, and could feel the gentle flow of the exhaust from our furnace. It was flowing right through my hand instead of around it. As I thought about that, I noticed that there was no sensation of heat from the fumes. In fact, when I got right down to it, I should have been freezing cold sitting out there on the roof. It was a pretty chilly night. There was no sensation of temperature at all.

With the top of the chimney only a few inches away from me, I noticed a name in the cement cap. **Nathan**. It looked as if it had been scratched in when the cement was wet.

Must have been one of the Tanner kids, when they built the house.

I looked around at the yard and at the roof again, and realized where I was. *What am I doing?* Being out of sight of my body caused me to panic. *How do I get back in? What if I can't get back in my body?*

I needn't have worried. I heard the familiar sound of Snap, Crackle, and Pop, and I was back with a jerk. The heartbeat was back. My chest was rising again. I flexed my fingers.

"Of course," I said out loud as I sat up in bed. "I THINK my way back, just like anywhere else." To assure myself that I was really whole again, I grabbed the clock and turned off the alarm.

Too cool! I said to myself as I settled back down. *I think I could get used to this.*

I fell asleep with a smile on my face.

CHAPTER 9

- Jumping Out -

When I woke up Saturday morning, it took a few minutes before I remembered the events of the previous night. Then I grinned as I reached over and reverently touched the clock on the nightstand.

Breakfast was just getting going when I went downstairs. On Saturdays we usually ate a late breakfast and an early supper. That way Mom only had two meals to worry about.

"How are you feeling this morning, Bart?" Mom asked, looking at my forehead.

"Huh? Oh, fine," I said. My nosedive in English seemed like a week ago already.

"What are your plans for today?" she asked.

"Well, I need to finish up my English report. It's due on Wednesday. Then, later on, I wanted to go over to Paul's house."

"That sounds fine. Paul seems like a nice boy. I'm glad you've been able to make friends so easily. Don't forget to do your chores first."

"Okay, Mom," I said.

I decided to read the last two books I had checked out. The one I picked up first turned out to be a documentary on a group of Indians in the southwest who claimed to have the ability to perform "astral projections" or "magic spirit separations"—to leave their bodies anytime they wanted. It was a religious sort of thing that took years of very intensive training to master. As I read some of their individual accounts, I was astounded to discover how similar their ability was to what had been happening to me—like controlling their destination by their thoughts and traveling at the speed of light all around the world.

I also learned that there was some sort of cord attached between the body and the spirit—like a magical, invisible bungee cord—that would stretch as far as you wanted it to go, but would always pull you back to your body.

That fits. I hadn't felt or seen any cord, but the effect of being jerked back by a giant rubber band was all too real. They mentioned that the only thing that would break or cut the cord was death.

Maybe I'm not so abnormal after all. Maybe all these NDEs aren't accidents at all. Maybe I could do it on purpose! Mind-boggling.

But how? What do I do to make it happen?

I spent the afternoon studying both books, but they were conveniently short on the how-to's. After grabbing a quick supper, I told my parents that I wasn't feeling well after all, and wanted to rest for a while.

"I'm going to close my door, so keep the noise down, please," I informed everybody. I shut myself in my room and closed the curtains. Not knowing what else to do, I lay on my bed, closed my eyes real tight, and clenched my fists in the air.

"Out!" I commanded out loud. Nothing happened. I reached over and grabbed the clock, just to make sure. "Still physical," I muttered. I got up, found a baseball, and sat it on the bed alongside of me.

Maybe I need to think it, instead of say it.

OUT! I thought, as forcefully as I could. I opened my eyes and grabbed the ball. "Junk!"

Maybe I need to tell myself where to go.

I chuckled. *Tell myself where to go. Good one.*

I squinted tight and tensed all up. *Paul's house! Paul's house! Paul's house!* I slowly opened one eye.

"Double junk!" I cussed, slamming the bed with both fists. "I don't get it." I put my hands behind my head and stared up at the ceiling.

Okay, let's think this out. Let's see . . . Last night when I jumped out . . . oh, yeah . . . there was a weird vibration first. In school, too. That's it! I thought excitedly. *I've got to vibrate first!*

Uh . . . sure, Bart. How do we vibrate? Shake all around on the bed? For lack of anything better, I tried it anyway. Anyone watching would have had me committed to the loony bin.

This is stupid. I don't have the foggiest idea how to do this. I turned over on my side and stared at the clock. After the seconds had counted up all the way from zero to fifty-nine, I turned back on my back, with my hands behind my head again. I decided to recall everything I could remember about all . . . how many times?

Five times! I counted. *No vibrations the first and second. Just pain. I don't want pain. Not sure about the accident. Mostly just raw fear. I don't want fear. That leaves yesterday. In class I was bored out of my gourd and trying hard to stay awake. Of course!* I realized at last. *Last night I was just about asleep when it happened. I have to go into a trance or something. It's like yoga.* I straightened my arms out stiffly alongside my body and shifted around to get comfortable.

Relax, relax, I told myself. *Just relax.* I closed my eyes and started taking deep breaths. After a few minutes, I could feel the muscles in my arms and legs loosen up.

Okay, relax the mind, too. I let my mind drift off on a few things, then caught myself. *I'm going to fall asleep if I don't watch it. I need to concentrate. I need to find the vibrations.*

And just like that, they started. It was as if they were just sitting there on the top of my head, waiting for me to look. All I had to do was let myself go, and they seemed to come all by themselves.

They're pulsing so fast this time, I can hardly feel them. They didn't bother me as much as the night before. In fact, it was very soothing and warm, like a heated vibrator bed.

Okay, UP! I willed myself. The vibrations stopped abruptly.

Dang! I cursed as I opened my eyes. *Still here, for Pete's sake. I had them! They were right here! What went wrong?* I sat up and grabbed the ball angrily from the bed. I was about to throw it into the closet when I realized I hadn't picked it up.

I tried again.

"YES!" I shouted. *"Yes! Yes! Yes! I'm out! I'm out! DOUBLE YES!"* I floated over and swung my arms deliberately through the dresser and the lamp, and did a karate kick through the window. Nothing moved.

This is great!

I looked down at the floor, closed my eyes, and imagined myself dropping into a swimming pool. I ended up in the living room right between Mom and Dad's chairs. They didn't even flinch.

Awesome!

Looking back up at the ceiling, I willed myself to rise. There I was, hovering over my own body on the bed. I quickly dropped back in, then physically leaped off the bed and started to do a dance around the room.

"Yahoo!" I yelled.

I just HAD to tell somebody, so I picked up my phone and called Paul. It rang forever, and I paced the floor like a caged animal.

"Come on, come on. Answer the phone."

Finally, "Hello?" It was Paul.

"Paul? Guess what! I've done it six times!"

"Done what? Who's this?"

"Jumped out! . . . of my body! I've been out six times! Can you believe it?"

There was a brief pause. "Bart, you're losing it."

"No, honest!" I yelled. Then I glanced at the door, remembering all the little ears in the house. "The last one was barely a minute ago," I whispered. "I did it on purpose, Paul! I figured it out!"

After another pause he said, "Let me get to another phone. Hang on." There was lots of background noise. "Okay, Mom. Hang it up!" he yelled. We both heard the click, but he waited.

"You there?" I asked.

"You had an NDE in English yesterday, didn't you?" he said accusingly. "Why didn't you tell me?"

"All right. I was rude, okay? I admit it. I was just worried that I was . . . mentally unbalanced or something. I got scared, that's all. It happened so fast—"

"Okay . . ." he cut in.

"Then last night, when I was just about asleep, I jumped out again." The volume of my voice started to rise. "I could see my body on the bed, Paul. Big as life. Then I floated right through the ceiling and sat on the roof!"

"You sure you weren't dreaming?"

"Positive! While I was up there, I saw this name scratched in the chimney. I climbed up on a ladder this morning to look. It was there, Paul. Just like I saw it last night. Do you know what this means?" I was practically hyperventilating.

"You said you had another one? A few minutes ago?" he asked, warming up.

"Yeah, that's the best part. I read these books today about some Indians that learned how to get out of their bodies any time they want. It's really cool. I got thinking that maybe I was using the same kind of ability. You know, doing it on purpose—subconsciously. So I lay down on the bed . . . and I figured it out!!"

"You mean you can leave your body on purpose?" he asked. "Whenever you want?"

"I think so. I've only done it once on purpose, so far." A brilliant idea popped into my head. "Hey, Paul. What do you say I try it again and see if I can get to your house?"

"You've GOT to be kidding," he whispered. "You want to come over to my house? . . . like invisible?" He was getting into it. "Now?"

"Yeah. Why not?"

"Go for it, man! This is too much!"

"Okay, I'll be there in a minute."

"Wait. What do I—?"

I slammed down the phone and hit the bed with a flying leap.

I tried everything, but could not get the vibrations to come. I tried deep breathing. I tried meditation. I tried watching the seconds on the clock. I tried desperately to get sleepy. Nothing worked. No vibrations. After about fifteen minutes, I called him back.

"Well?" he asked, expectantly.

"It didn't work," I said.

"What do you mean, it didn't work?"

"I couldn't get out. I think I'm too hyped up."

"Well, try it again!" he pleaded.

"It's no good, Paul. I've got to calm down first. I'm going to take a cold shower and try again later. I'll call you." I wasn't sure who was more disappointed—him or me.

After the shower and a snack break in the kitchen, I went back to bed. I still couldn't jump out. My mind was racing, and hundreds of thoughts competed for time in my head.

My hand melting through the clock . . . the accident . . . the chimney . . . trying to go to Paul's . . . falling out in English.

I can't wait to tell Roshayne, I thought excitedly. *Now she'll believe.*

Of course the thought of one pretty girl inevitably led to another. *I wonder what Tiffany would think of my jumping out . . . dang, she's good looking!*

I was enjoying visualizing the last time I had seen her walk down the hall—actually I was mentally gawking—when I felt the vibrations start again.

Oh, boy! Here they come! I waited a few seconds for them to get going. I had barely completed the thought, *Out,* when I felt a weird kind of . . . head rush.

When I opened my eyes, I was staring at a big velvet curtain, five feet in front of me.

CHAPTER 10

- The Snatch -

What the heck—? Where am I—?

"That's her, arriving at school," a voice said behind me.

I spun around and found myself looking over the shoulder of some guy in a big chair at a desk. There were two other men standing on the other side. The one talking was a giant—and I mean HUMONGOUS—bodybuilder-type dude. He was pointing at a picture on the desk.

How in the heck did I get here? I've got to get out of here.

"Tell me about her," replied the man in the chair. He picked up the photograph.

"She's seventeen years old," said the bodybuilder.

My ears perked up. *Seventeen years old?*

"She has a pretty tight routine up until about five o'clock. She usually rides to school with her boyfriend." He leaned over the desk again, pointing to another photo. "That's him on the right. Name's Randy. They eat lunch together at school."

Boy, she's a fox, I thought, hovering over the desk.

"Classes are over at two-thirty. Most days, she stays late doing student council or something. She hitches a ride home with one of the other kids if the boyfriend isn't around. In the evenings she comes and goes a lot, but nothing regular."

I wonder what this is all about.

"What about the weekends?"

"She usually has dates Friday and Saturday nights. Sunday is going to be our best bet. We've watched her for three weeks now. Her family lives a block and a half away from their church, and they all walk. The chick is always late and goes by herself."

"Are you proposing we do this snatch in broad daylight?" he asked, looking back and forth at the two. "In the middle of her own neighborhood?"

"Yes, sir."

This snatch? What on earth are they talking about?

"Is very easy," the other man said. He was a middle-aged Indian with a nearly black complexion, long braided gray hair, and a badly scarred face. His hands, wrists, and neck were loaded down with silver and turquoise. "Whole neighborhood is in church at same time. I have seen in many houses these three weeks. Always empty for three hours' time."

The man in the chair contemplated that for a few moments while the two men stood quietly waiting.

"My powers do not mistake," added the Indian softly.

His powers?

"Tell me more about her father," he said, apparently satisfied.

"Forty-two years old. Good health," answered the bodybuilder. "Appears to be happily married. Four other children, all younger boys. They live up on the east side, in the foothills. Chief executive officer and principal stockholder of his company."

What does her father have to do with anything?

"What kind of company?"

"They sell sporting goods and have franchises all over the country. He's a self-made multi-millionaire. They just sold off a new block of franchises in the mid-west and have plans for more in the near future. They are cash heavy right now. But we'll need to move quickly, before it gets re-invested."

"How heavy?"

"From what Hawk has seen on their computers, I'd say in the neighborhood of nine to ten million. Maybe more."

Ten million? Cash? Dollars?

"Nine or ten million," he repeated, leaning back in his chair, his fingertips together. "Very good. Very good indeed."

There's something very wrong here.

"What about his schedule?"

"As regular as a clock," answered the bodybuilder. "Silver Hawk has been watching him in his office now for two weeks solid. No plans for leaving town anytime soon. I've been tailing him after he leaves work, and shooting photos."

"Okay, they'll do fine," he announced, leaning forward over the desk. "Let's take her tomorrow."

Take her? I echoed.

"Tomorrow?" questioned the bodybuilder. His cast-in-stone face cracked just a fraction.

"Tomorrow's Sunday, isn't it? Aren't you ready?"

"Yes, Mr. Clawson," he answered quickly. "Whenever you say the word."

"Very good," Clawson replied. "Give me the rundown."

"We'll be using an old Chevy van we found up north last week. Hawk will drive, and I'll scoop her up. It'll be a cakewalk."

"It had better be. Make sure you're disguised and the van is properly disposed of."

"Everything is in order. No need to worry."

If I didn't know better, I'd say these guys were planning a kidnapping or something.

"Where are you going to keep her?" asked Clawson.

"I have an old house in the downtown area," the bodybuilder answered. "Paid cash for it three years ago. Dead-end street. Lots of trees and bushes. Neighbors stay to themselves. I've used it as a safe house a few times."

Oh my gosh! They ARE planning a kidnapping!

"Perfect. Okay, Derek, you'll be baby-sitting her most of the time, but make sure you can keep her securely locked up, in case I need you. Stock up on food and supplies, and just stay put 'til I call."

"Consider it done."

I've got to do something!

He turned to the Indian. "Hawk, after the snatch I'll need you to do your magic on Fenton and report to me regularly. We'll let him stew for a day, then we'll call on Monday afternoon. He should be pretty rattled by then. Let me know as soon as you have her chained down, and we can finalized my plans for the handoff."

"Yes, sir," they answered in unison.

They're going to hold her for ransom!

"That'll be all."

Derek and Silver Hawk turned and left the office.

After the door closed, Mr. Clawson unlocked the left drawer of his desk and pulled out a thin black book. Turning to the first page, he began writing.

What am I going to do? These guys are really going to kidnap that girl! I've got to tell somebody!

I was so busy thinking and worrying that it didn't occur to me, until it was too late, to see what he was writing. Clawson closed the book and returned it to the drawer, along with all the photos. That done, he locked the drawer and pocketed the key.

Leaning back in his chair, he chuckled. "You're going to make me a wealthy man, sweetheart."

Suddenly I felt a strong tugging sensation, and I was pulled, instantly and uncontrollably, back to my body. When I opened my eyes, Darin was shaking me violently.

"Wake up, Bart! Come on! Wake up!" He was nearly hysterical.

"Okay, already," I snapped. "I'm back." He stepped away, confused. "Awake, I mean. I'm awake. What's the matter?"

"Mom just wanted me to tell you that Paul called," he said. "Boy, Bart, I've never seen anybody sleep like that. I thought you were dead or something." He turned and ran from the room.

As soon as he was gone, I jumped for the phone—not to call Paul, though. My finger jabbed furiously at the buttons. Before it could ring, I hung up.

What am I doing? I can't call the police. I don't know who they are. There could be a thousand Mr. Clawsons around here.

Wait a minute! Around where? I don't even know where I was. I could have been in Salt Lake, for all I knew. Or New York!

I lay down heavily on the bed. I had never felt so totally helpless in my whole life.

CHAPTER 11

- *Paul* -

Paul sat by me in Sunday School class and impatiently whispered, "You never called. What happened?"

"I got sidetracked," I whispered back.

"What do you mean, 'sidetracked'? Did you jump out or not?"

"Yeah, I did."

"And?"

"I ended up in somebody's office somehow."

"Somebody's office? Why'd you do that?"

"I didn't do it on purpose."

"So, are you going to try again tonight?"

"I guess so."

"What time are you going to come?"

"I don't know. It depends on what we're doing," I answered. "Tell you what. You just do whatever you do, and I'll try when I can. That way we can compare notes later about what you were doing and what I saw. Okay?"

"Cool."

After church, Mom kept me busy helping prepare dinner, and I had absolutely no chance of getting off by myself. I thought about calling the police again, but couldn't come up with anything believable to tell them.

Hello, Police? Somewhere in the country, a guy named Clawson and his two friends are going to kidnap a seventeen-year-old girl! You've go to do something!

Sure, kid. Thanks for calling.

I wondered if I could somehow find the bad guys, but I had no clue where they were, or how I got there in the first place. I was afraid to lie down anyway, even for a few minutes, for fear someone would come and interrupt me. It wouldn't do to have them find my body looking like warmed-over death again. It was well after nine o'clock before we finished up with all our family stuff, and I was finally able to slip away.

"I'm going to my room now," I told Mom. "See you in the morning."

"Good night, Bart," Mom and Dad both answered back. I hurriedly got ready for bed, then closed the door all the way and turned off the light.

At last I was ready. I decided the best way to relax was to lie flat on my back, with my hands and arms at my side. I closed my eyes and forced myself to relax.

It was just like the night before. I was too tense and anxious about jumping out, and just couldn't clear my mind.

Somehow, I've got to think of something else. A scene from a cartoon came to mind about sheep jumping over a fence. *What have I got to lose?* I asked myself.

So I started counting. That worked pretty well, and after about two hundred fifty or so, I could feel my muscles settling down and my breathing going slower. By the time I got to four hundred, it felt almost like I didn't have a body from the neck down. After about five hundred, my mind started to wander away from sheep to other things, and I realized I was getting close to drifting off to sleep.

This is as relaxed as I'm going to get. I remembered the weird vibrations that seemed to happen before jumping out. Making a conscious effort not to move or breathe too deeply, I replayed the feeling and amazingly brought on the vibrations almost automatically. The pulsing through my body felt soothing, warm and gentle, and even faster than the night before. Almost too fast to even feel the vibrations.

As they flowed, I began thinking, *Paul's house. Paul's house.* The rhythm continued uninterrupted, and I remembered that I needed to command or think myself out of my body first.

Up, I commanded myself. The rhythm stopped, and I was on the ceiling.

I didn't even bother looking down at my body.

Paul's house, I thought.

No sooner thought than done. The mile or so of cornfields separating our two houses raced by in a dark blur, and I was standing in a lighted room. I recognized it immediately as Paul's bedroom. Paul was sitting at his desk, working on his airplane, meticulously applying a decal to the right side of the fuselage.

I moved over by his side. *"Hey, Paul,"* I said out loud. *"I made it!."* He didn't pay any attention.

I yelled right in his ear. *"Paul! Can you hear me?"* Not so much as a twitch.

I decided I'd better take note of how he was dressed and how things were arranged in his room.

Of course, if I tell him all about his room, he could call it a lucky guess, I realized. *I've seen all this stuff already.*

I maneuvered myself to different places around the room, trying to find something that I hadn't seen before. I was standing with my back to the door when I suddenly heard the door being opened. I knew I was going to get clobbered, but before I could move out of the way, the door went through my back and right out my front. It was very unnerving.

But the real shock came when I discovered that the doorknob was still connected to a hand, which was connected to an arm, which was immediately followed by an entire person passing right through me and stopping just a few inches in front of my nose.

I jumped quickly to the side. Even after the chimney and the ceilings, floors, and walls, it had never occurred to me that I could go through PEOPLE. Even worse, that they could go through ME!

"It's getting to be about bedtime, Paul," his mom said. "Tomorrow's a school day, you know."

"I know, Mom. I was just finishing up these decals while I was waiting for Bart to call."

"Well, maybe he got busy. I'm sure you can talk to him tomorrow at school."

"Yeah, I guess so."

"Good night, dear."

"Good night, Mom."

I've got to hurry back so I can call him before he goes to bed

I had forgotten that he was going to be waiting all afternoon for me to come.

Back to body, I thought. Going back seemed to happen a lot faster than going out, and I was snapped back so violently that I gasped out loud from the impact. I jumped from the bed and went to the phone.

"Hello?"

"Hi, Mrs. Bishop. Is Paul there?" Of course, I knew he was there.

"Yes, he is. Is this Bart?" she asked.

"Yes, ma'am."

"He's been expecting your call. Just a minute and I'll get him."

Paul came on the line, and his mom hung up. "Bart? Don't tell me. You've been trying all afternoon, and it still didn't work. Right?"

"Well, actually it did," I said excitedly.

"It did?"

"Yeah. I was just there."

"You were? In my room?"

"Yeah, can you believe it?"

"Jeez! So . . . what am I wearing?"

"Your dark blue pants, a white shirt—untucked, with no tie—and stocking feet."

He gasped audibly over the phone. "What else did you see?"

"You were sticking a decal on your remote control airplane."

"No way!" he said breathlessly.

"Then, I was standing right in front of your door when your mom came in and told you to get to bed."

"No way, Bart! That was just seconds ago!"

"Well, I travel pretty fast out-of-body." I related back to him verbatim their short conversation. "But get this. She walked right THROUGH me. She scared me to death."

"Get out! Bart, this is too cool. I can't believe you did it. Why didn't you talk to me?" he asked.

"I yelled right in your ear, but you didn't even flinch."

"Hang on a sec." He covered the phone and talked to somebody. "I've got to get to bed, Bart. My mom's getting upset."

"Okay, we can talk more tomorrow."

"You're not going to come back tonight, are you?" he asked nervously.

"No. Why would I?"

"Promise? I don't much like the idea of you hanging around

here all night when I can't even see you."

"I promise, don't worry. I'll see you tomorrow."

After hanging up the phone, I lay back down on my bed and studied the ceiling.

Is this cool, or what? I thought. *I can jump out just about anytime I want, just as easy as climbing out of bed.*

I chuckled to myself. *Paul's worried about me spying on him.* I closed my eyes and starting daydreaming about haunting his house—like making spooky noises, or causing pictures to fall off the walls. *Too bad this isn't like the movies. I could REALLY have some fun.*

Then I realized how shortsighted I was. Paul's wasn't the only house in the world. *I could spy on just about anybody I wanted to. They would never even know I was there!* I started to get real excited. *I could drop in on my cousins in California in five seconds flat. I could go to the movies and concerts without paying. I could go to the Super Bowl without paying! . . . and stand right on the fifty yard line! . . . in the middle of the field! Wow!*

I could hear what people are saying about me behind my back. Especially the girls! That'd be cool.

I was so caught up in the euphoria of the moment that I hardly even noticed the warm feeling that came over my body.

I could stand right by their lockers and hear their whole conversation, I continued. *I wonder where Roshayne's locker is, anyway.*

Whoosh! All of a sudden I was standing in the air, looking down from the ceiling. Only I wasn't in my bedroom.

Oh, great! Where am I now?

There was a single bed in the center of the floor, and a nightstand, dresser, and vanity against the walls. The room was dark, but I had the same night vision that I had experienced the night of the accident.

How did I get here? Looking around the room and not seeing anything familiar left me a little uneasy. *This is getting out of hand. I could be anywhere.* I started to panic.

Something moved, and I was shocked to see that there was a person in the bed.

Roshayne! I gasped in horror. *What am I doing in Roshayne's bedroom?* Then I relaxed and smiled. *I'm in Roshayne's bedroom. Cool.*

Curiosity took over. *It's not like she's indecent or anything. And she'll never even know I'm here.* I felt like the ultimate Peeping Tom, but I didn't let it bother me too much.

I slowly surveyed the room. *Sure is a girly looking place,* I mused. The walls were papered with a violet and pink flowery pattern. The curtains were thick, with tassels and trim. There was a china doll standing on an embroidered doily on top of the dresser, with a music box on one side and a vase with a silk rose on the other. The vanity was neatly arranged with assorted items of makeup, perfume, and jewelry. The bedspread matched the curtains. The headboard and footboard were a rosewood color and had tall, round, tapering posts rising high from each corner—like for a canopy bed, but without the canopy.

I moved over to the edge of the bed to get a closer look at Roshayne. She was sleeping on her back with both arms out of the covers, hands clasped loosely over her stomach. She was wearing a light flannel-looking pajama, with long sleeves and laced cuffs, and a high buttoned-up collar. I studied her face for a few minutes. Her delicate features hypnotized me. Her eyelashes looked longer than ever with her eyes closed. Her hair was fanned out beautifully on the pillow on either side. There was just a hint of a smile on her face, as though she was enjoying a pleasant dream. She looked so peaceful and sweet—like Sleeping Beauty.

"Roshayne, you are the most beautiful creature I have ever set eyes on," I told her. It was great fun, being able to say whatever I wanted and knowing she couldn't hear me. *"I'd give anything to be able to touch you right now."*

I just couldn't help myself. I reached down and tenderly, carefully caressed her right cheek with the back of my forefinger. Even with my spirit finger, it felt soft.

"I think I love you, Rosh."

Just then she drew a deep breath, which she let out slowly. I backed away. Her right hand came to her cheek, placing two fingertips on the exact spot that I had been caressing. Her lips moved, then settled into a pleasant smile.

Was it my imagination? I thought, startled, *or did I just see her mouth the word "Bart"?*

I stood there in shock. *How was it possible?*

CHAPTER 12

- Mistake -

Waking up Monday morning, I was surprised at how rested and refreshed I felt. I was afraid that after doing all that jumping out-of-body, I would be exhausted. I whistled happily all through breakfast, and Mom started to wonder what was up.

"He probably dreamed about that Roshayne chick all night," Darin volunteered.

I could feel my face turn red. "Shut up, you little twerp," I yelled at him, giving him my meanest I'll-kill-you-later look. Mom just smiled and looked at me, amused.

You don't know how right you are, Darin, I thought to myself.

"Hey, Mom," I said, changing the subject. "Now that I have my own license, I was wondering if it would be okay to use the car Friday night. I have a date for the homecoming dance."

"Here we go again," she muttered. Then she looked at me sweetly and said, "Of course, Bart. There's no sense putting it off. We'll just have to get used to the fact that we have another licensed driver in the family. Who are you taking to the dance?"

"Uh . . . Roshayne Pennini," I answered nervously. Darin chuckled, and I kicked him in the shin under the table.

"Remember," Mom said, "we have a rule against single dating until you graduate from high school."

"I know, Mom. Paul and I are going to double. He's taking Tamara Edmonds."

"Who?"

"You know . . . the girl who broke her arm in the accident?"

"Oh. Tammy," she said, turning back to her dishwashing. "She's a nice girl. I like her."

"We were originally planning to go as an eightsome, but Neil won't go anywhere without Jill, and Scott couldn't find a date," I explained between bites of pancakes. "Or wouldn't. I'm not sure if he ever actually asked anybody. He's kind of shy with girls."

"Scott's the one—"

"—who wore the seat belt," I echoed sarcastically. "Right."

"How's Jill doing, anyway?" she asked in a sort of here-comes-a-lecture tone of voice.

"Still in a coma," I answered hesitantly, wondering where the conversation was heading.

"Well, just be sure you drive carefully, obey the traffic laws, and stay in town," she cautioned, pointing a soapy finger at me. "That accident happened because a car full of crazy teenagers went on a joyride after a dance. We don't want any repeat performances, now do we?"

"We'll be fine, Mom. Don't worry." I knew she would anyway. After all, that's what Moms are for, right?

During study time, I went to the library to find Paul. He was nowhere in sight, but Roshayne was there. I pulled up a chair. "Mind if I sit here?"

She looked up and smiled. "Oh, hi, Bart. No. Go right ahead." She went back to what she was reading. I just sat there, soaking in her smile. After a moment's silence, she glanced up and caught me staring at her.

"Don't you have any homework to do?" she whispered with a smile. "You're making me nervous, staring at me like that." I grinned and kept on staring anyway.

"Bart, what's WRONG with you? If you don't knock it off, I'm going to go sit somewhere else," she threatened, still smiling.

"I've done it nine times now, Rosh," I announced.

"Done what?"

"I've jumped out of my body now a total of nine times. Six of them just since last Friday."

"What are you saying?"

"I have the ability to get my spirit out of my body—to astral project."

"Astral what? What are you talking about?"

I leaned farther across the table and lowered my whisper. "Rosh, it is the most wonderful thing you can ever imagine! I can get right out of my body and float around invisible anytime I want! Isn't that cool?"

She closed her book and furrowed her eyebrows. "Explain," she demanded.

"Did you hear what happened to me Friday in English?"

"Somebody said you passed out and hit your head." She looked up at my forehead, where there was still a pretty good purple bruise.

"I didn't pass out. I JUMPED out!" I said excitedly. "Only I didn't do it on purpose. I fell asleep sitting at my desk, and next thing you know—WHAM!—my body fell right off me and crashed on my desk. It scared me to death. In fact, it took me a few seconds to realize what had happened."

"Bart, are you for real?" she asked.

"Scout's honor," I said, holding up three fingers. "Then Friday night, while I was thinking about it, I jumped out again." I told her all about the clock and the ceiling and the chimney. "I even climbed up on a ladder Saturday morning to find the name." She leaned forward, resting her chin in both hands. She was so close I could feel her breath on my face.

"On Saturday I read all about separating the spirit from the body on purpose, and I figured out how to do it on my own." I told her about floating through the roof, and about the trips to the mystery office and to Paul's house.

"This is unbelievable, Bart," she said. After thinking it over a little, she asked, "When were the other times?"

"Huh?" It suddenly occurred to me that my count had included the visit to her room.

"That was only five," she said. "Two on Friday, two on Saturday, and one yesterday."

"Oh," I said, somewhat relieved. "Remember, I told you about the time in third grade? When I was in the hospital? And the accident, of course."

"I thought you said those were NDEs."

"Well, I assumed they were. But I think I just subconsciously jumped out both times. There was another time in fifth grade that I just remembered about, a couple of days ago. I had an accident at camp, and jumped out while I was in the ambulance on the way to the hospital."

Her mind was going at top speed, trying to analyze all the information I had thrown at her. "So, you claim you can just jump out or . . . what did you call it . . . project? Any time you want?"

"Did you tell her?" a boy's voice said right next to me.

I about jumped out of my skin. "Criminy, Paul. Did you have to sneak up on me like that? You scared me to death!"

"He told me," Roshayne answered. "Do YOU believe him?"

"Oh, yeah," he said, nodding vigorously. "After what he said he saw me doing last night, I believe him, all right. He came to my house. Did he tell you?"

"Yeah, he did." She looked back at me and asked suspiciously, "So what about the other one?"

"Other one?" my voiced squeaked a little.

"You haven't told me about the ninth one," she reminded me.

I fidgeted and started twisting my ring around my finger. "Maybe . . . I miscounted."

"Bart, you're hiding something. Tell me about—"

"I didn't go on purpose, Rosh," I blurted out. "You've got to believe me. It just happened."

"What—?" she started.

"I was thinking about school and lockers and girls, and just when the vibrations came, I was thinking about you, and then—"

She slapped her hands down hard on the table and stood up real slow. "You went to my house?!" she said, slow and accusing, putting her hands on her hips. If looks could kill, I would have been vaporized. "Well, I . . . ! This is . . . ! I don't . . . !" she stammered.

"Sit down, Rosh, and let me explain."

"Yeah, sit down, Rosh," Paul echoed. "You're going to get us in trouble here."

"Bart's already in big trouble, mister!" she said heatedly. Turning back to me, she demanded, "What were you doing in my house?"

"I was trying to tell you," I said, lowering my voice. "I got there because I thought of YOU, not your house. My thoughts seem to be connected to some kind of built-in automatic navigation system that finds whoever I'm thinking about. I think 'Paul,' and I'm flying over cornfields to Paul's house. During the accident, I thought 'Mom and Dad,' and I was instantly home. Last night, all I thought was 'I wonder where Roshayne's locker is,' and I was suddenly in your bedroom. My subconscious mind just homed in on you."

Her faced turned beet red. "My BEDROOM?" she screeched, her voice about an octave higher than usual. She grabbed her books off the table. "Don't you ever, EVER do that again, you twisted, demented . . . !" She stormed off toward the door.

"Gosh, Bart," Paul said to me, as we turned back to the table, "I can't believe you went into her bedroom. What were you thinking?"

"I didn't do it on purpose," I repeated.

"Well, you've got to admit, it makes you look pretty guilty, going in a girl's bedroom at night and all." He stood up. "I've got to finish my report. I'll see you later."

"Yeah, later," I answered.

With my back to the door, I didn't see her come back. She dropped her books heavily on the table and sat back down, staring holes in me for several seconds.

"What did you see?" she demanded.

"You were in bed, sleeping," I answered. "That's all."

"In bed. Sleeping," she mimicked.

"Yeah, sleeping."

"What time was it?"

"I don't know. Almost ten, maybe."

She regarded me coolly for a moment. "You're going to have to do a lot better than that, Bart," she said finally, "because I don't believe you. Convince me. What does my room look like?"

I swallowed hard and told her everything I had seen. I described the curtains and the bed, and all the things on the furniture and walls. I even described her pajamas. She mellowed a little as I went, but still wasn't absolutely convinced. She pressed me for more details. Things like what color the doll's dress was, what jewelry I saw on the vanity, and stuff like that.

"You really were there, weren't you?" she said finally, with a look of genuine shock on her face.

The bell rang, and it was time to go to history.

"This is all pretty unbelievable, you know," she said as we left the library.

"I'm just as surprised as you are, believe me."

She thought some more on the way down the hall. "If you can really do what you say you can do . . ." she paused, " . . . it opens up a whole world of possibilities."

"I've been going crazy for days, just thinking about it," I replied.

She was quiet again, until we reached the seminary building. "Okay," she conceded. "I'm going to have to believe you, I guess. But I'm going to need a little time to get used to it."

"That's okay," I answered.

"I'm sorry I got mad at you," she whispered as we entered the classroom, "but you're going to have to be more careful what you think about, if you're going to go flying all over the place."

Isn't that the truth.

At the dinner table, Dad read us an article from the evening paper about a girl from Provo who had been kidnapped and was being held for ransom.

"They grabbed her on her way to church," he said. "Can you believe that?"

"Church? In Provo?" I asked, sitting up. "What's her name?"

He scanned the article. "Andrea."

Could it be? I wondered.

"Unbelievable," Mom said. "I thought we left that kind of thing behind us. What's this world coming to when you can't even walk to church in your own neighborhood?"

"The kidnappers are asking for three millions dollars," Dad continued. "Apparently her father is pretty wealthy."

Oh my gosh! It is! "Excuse me," I said. "I'm going to my room."

"Was it something I said?" Dad joked.

I jumped up and hurried out of the kitchen.

Three million dollars! Holy smokes!

In my room, I made another frantic attempt at calling the police, then hung up again just as fast. I sat down hard and slammed the desk with my fist.

How would I explain to the police how I overheard that meeting? I thought desperately. *I still don't know who they are, or where they are.*

This is horrible! I witnessed a kidnapping in the making, and I can't even do anything about it.

I had nightmares all night about the bodybuilder and the Indian.

Tuesday morning, walking into the school, I was dying to tell Paul about the kidnapping.

Before I could open my mouth, he said, "You know, Bart, I've been thinking about your jumping out and stuff."

"Jeeze, Paul," I whispered. "Not so loud. You want the whole world to know?"

"You said you could go anywhere you want, right?"

"Yeah."

"And nobody can see you or hear you, right?"

"Yeah, so?"

He paused. "So, you could walk right through the girls' locker room and nobody would see you. Right?"

"What?!" I stopped dead in my tracks. I couldn't believe what I had just heard. Actually it wasn't so much what, as who. I wouldn't have been surprised at all to hear my California friends say something like that. *But Paul's . . . different!*

"Paul! I would NEVER do that. I can't believe you would even suggest such a thing."

He glared at me, then turned and hurried off. "Well, I would if I could," he called back over his shoulder.

That's why God didn't give YOU the gift, I thought disgustedly. Something clicked.

The gift. This is the gift. Something precious and rare, I remembered as I walked to my locker.

Tiffany was just closing her locker when I got there.

"Hi, Tiff," I said, risking the use of her nickname.

"Hi, Bart. What's up?"

"Oh, nothing," I answered. "You know."

"Yeah." She turned and walked away, wiggling her hips. "See ya."

Wow! She actually acknowledged my existence. And she even remembered my name. Cool! I reveled in the moment.

During study hall, I retired to my favorite place in the building. Some energetic guys, years before, had gone to the trouble of carrying an old couch all the way up the stairs and through the catwalks to the light room. It made a great place for tech crew visitors to watch assemblies and productions. Best seats in the house. It also made for a secure and isolated place for me to hide out, without having to worry about interruptions.

I relaxed on the couch and summoned the vibrations, and they came in less than a minute. I concentrated on staying in the light room as I jumped out. That worked well, and I was soon hovering over the control panel.

I spent several minutes after that moving around the hallways in the school and going in and out of classrooms. I zigzagged my way through one room, passing through everyone's body, including the teacher's. One girl shivered as I went through her. That was neat.

Walking slowly through walls with my eyes open was weird. It would go a little dark as I went through, but not so much that I couldn't see the block and mortar. And everything was in perfect focus, even right against my eyeballs.

Going down the halls, the long rows of lockers caught my attention, and I went through about fifty of them, one after the other.

There are no secrets, I boasted to myself. *I see all and know all!*

I decided to experiment with projecting myself somewhere else, like I'd done to Paul's. *Huish Theater,* I commanded myself. I didn't even try to slow down and arrived in a split second, hovering right in the middle of the street in front of the theater. *That's pretty cool,* I thought, as a big tow truck drove right through me. *Now, slowly. Back to the school.*

After moving three or four blocks over the downtown area, I thought of Paul for some reason, and was suddenly standing over his shoulder in the library. He was busy finishing up some research for his report. I remembered what had happened between us that morning, and realized how little I really knew about him.

I can't believe he suggested walking through the girls' locker room. Still, I smiled, *it WOULD be pretty excit—*

Mistake.

Another blur of motion and there I was—standing in the hall facing a pair of double doors with the sign "Girls' Gymnasium" on one of them. Of course, that was as close to the actual locker room as I had ever been, so that was where my built-in homing device took me.

Boy, that was close, I thought with a sigh of relief. *Only a few more feet through that wall, and I would have been right in—*
Another mistake.

I was abruptly surrounded by thick rising steam and the sounds of girls' voices all around me—and the sight of a whole lot more than I should have been seeing. I gasped, hurriedly closed my eyes, and shouted to myself, *BACK TO BODY!!*

I lay there on the couch in the light room for a long time after that, trembling and sweating. I was totally overcome with guilt.

What have I done? I cried. *I've committed a terrible sin!* The mental anguish pressed down on me like a giant boulder, and I bawled like a baby for several minutes, struggling with my conscience.

You idiot, Paul! I hate you for putting that thought in my head!

I made no attempt to get to history class, and was barely able to pull myself together in time to catch the bus. I hung around at the end of the line until almost everyone was on, then hurried and sat in the first available seat. I did NOT want to sit by Paul or Roshayne. Or Scott or Neil, or anybody else I knew. I was sure they would see "Guilty" written all over my face.

My appetite was gone, so I skipped dinner and barricaded myself in my room. After two or three hours of punishing myself, I remembered that my English paper was due the next day. Working on that helped get my mind off my trouble, but it was difficult concentrating enough to finish it up. When it was time for bed, I hurriedly crawled deep under the covers, as though I could hide from God. I tossed and turned miserably all night long.

On Wednesday, we started presenting our oral reports to the class. We drew numbers to see who would go first, and I drew the last slot for the first day. Paul drew the first slot for the last day. I saw him heave a sigh of relief and concluded that he probably hadn't quite finished his paper. Sooner than I expected, it was my turn. I stood and faced the class, full of fear and trepidation.

"My report is on Near Death Experiences and Out-of-Body Experiences. NDEs and OBEs." Just saying the words brought another flood of guilt to my mind, and I had to stop for a second to clear my throat and find my voice again. It was all I could do to keep from running out of the room.

Somehow I managed. When I finished, I handed my report to the teacher and returned to my desk, just as the bell rang. Several kids commented about what a cool report it was as they left. Paul gave me a high-five on his way out. I returned it, but not very enthusiastically.

As I was leaving, a girl calling my name stopped me. I turned around to see her cautiously approaching, as if she was afraid of me. She was short and a little plump, and wore really thick glasses. I didn't remember her name.

She stopped and waited for the room to clear. "You had one, didn't you?"

I didn't want to admit that I had, but I didn't want to lie, either. My silence was enough.

"In that car accident?" she asked.

"Yes," I admitted.

Her eyes started to water. "I had no idea there were so many other people who have had experiences like that. I've been so alone for so long."

"What do you mean?" I asked.

She tried hard to fight back her tears. "I had one myself," she confessed, "two years ago. I told my parents about it, and they said I was crazy. I told a couple of my friends, and they said I was nuts, too. They've hardly talked to me since. I even told my boyfriend, and he told me I was probably dreaming or hallucinating. Everybody thinks I'm crazy. I've just about convinced myself that I really AM crazy."

"I'm glad you told me," I responded. By then, I was having trouble with my own eyes.

"It really helps me to know someone else who's had one," she said, sniffling.

"Me, too," I said.

She took her glasses off to wipe her eyes. "Thank you so much, Bart." She smiled and headed for the door. Turning back, she added, "I'm going to read those books you found at the library. Maybe I can start living my life again." She left.

"You will be a great blessing to many people." Ol' Lady Owens' words came forcefully into my mind.

That night at the dinner table, Dad gave us an update.

"You'll never believe what I heard on the radio today," he said. "That kidnapped girl's father came up with the three million dollars in cash by yesterday afternoon and insisted on storing it in his private safe in his house overnight. Apparently, they were supposed to do a handoff someplace today. Well, when he went to his safe this morning to get the money, he found the vault door wide open and his daughter sitting inside—bound, gagged, and blindfolded. Of course, the money was gone. The two cops, who were supposedly guarding the safe, were both unconscious on the family room floor."

I closed my eyes and breathed a long sigh. *She's safe! What a relief!*

I tried over and over Wednesday night to jump out. Nothing would happen. I tried again during lunch and study hall, and all evening Thursday without results. Same thing all day Friday. I couldn't figure out what I was doing wrong.

In history class, Ol' Lady Owens' words unexpectedly pricked my conscience. *"If you are selfish or use it thoughtlessly, the Lord will withdraw it from you."*

Oh no! I thought. I was suddenly afraid that God might have taken away the gift for good. *Please, don't let it be so!*

As soon as I got off the bus, I locked myself in the upstairs bathroom, knelt clumsily by the side of the tub, and prayed like I had never prayed before. I pleaded with God to forgive me. I begged him to help me control my thoughts and actions, and to exercise wisdom in how I used the gift. I urged him to give it back, and promised that I would use it only to bless others.

When I came out, it felt as though a heavy load had been lifted from my shoulders. I knew all was well. With my conscience finally at ease, my appetite caught up with me—just in time for my big First Date.

CHAPTER 13

~ Witnesses ~

We ate in a nice restaurant on the highway going toward the neighboring town of Spanish Fork, and it was just after dusk when we headed back into Payson. Our route to the dance took us through a six-block section of the downtown area that had somehow missed out on all the upgrading and development that had been going on around town. It was in a low, hollow-like area, and as we dropped down into it we left behind the sidewalks, curbs, and streetlights. The houses were older and farther apart, with gravel driveways. The entire area was heavily wooded. Some local residents still kept horses and other animals in corrals behind their homes.

It looked like a fun place for kids to play in during the day, but a pretty spooky place to be at night.

I was driving the family car, with Roshayne sitting to my right. Paul was sitting in the backseat with Tamara. We were busy discussing the various school activities going on, and were anxious to get to the dance.

By sheer coincidence, at that exact moment, a car pulled into a driveway on the opposite street, its headlights shining briefly through the block of trees. For that brief instant, the flash of light created a perfect silhouette of three people in the woods who otherwise would have been totally hidden in the darkness. Tamara had been absentmindedly watching out her window, when suddenly she drew in a sharp breath and twisted around, staring into the woods.

"Omagosh," she said under her breath. "Omagosh! Omagosh!" she cried out a little louder.

"What's the matter?" asked Roshayne, turning around to see. Tamara started bouncing up and down in her seat, then spun around to the front.

"You guys, stop the car!" she yelled. "Omagosh!" She turned back and stared out the back window.

I thought we must have run over a dog or something. I let my foot off the gas and was about to brake when she spun around again in a panic.

"NOT HERE!" she shouted. "Go down to the corner!"

She looked terrified, so I did as she asked. She quickly turned back around again, kneeling on the seat and staring intently out the back window.

"What's going on?" I asked irritably as I pulled the car to a stop.

"Tammy, what on earth's the matter?" Roshayne asked. "What happened?" We were all trying to find whatever it was she was looking at.

"You guys!" Tamara said in a hoarse whisper. "I think I just saw somebody getting beat up!"

"Oh, come on," I said.

"Are you kidding?" Paul asked sarcastically.

"Does it look like I'm kidding?" Tamara screamed at him.

"Where?" I asked.

"Right back there in the trees," she said, pointing.

Paul and I looked out the back, then at each other.

Girls.

"What exactly did you see, Tammy?" asked Roshayne.

"It looked like two guys beating up on somebody. They had sticks or knives or something in their hands."

We all looked at her for a second.

"I think your imagination is going haywire," I said. "You probably just saw some kids playing around."

"We've got to DO something!" she insisted, ignoring me.

"Like what?" asked Paul. "You want us to go and check it out?"

She didn't answer, so Paul and I both opened our doors at the same time to get out.

"NO!" she screamed, pulling Paul back in the car. "They might be dangerous!"

"Then, what?" he demanded, closing his door.

"Yeah, what are we supposed do?" echoed Roshayne.

Tamara sat back and sobbed. "I don't know."

"Well, it's obvious we're not going to get to the dance until we clear this up," I said. "I have an idea."

They all looked at me expectantly.

"I'll go back by myself and look . . . out-of-body. That way there's no danger."

Roshayne smiled. "Good idea."

"You can do that?" asked Paul. "From right here?"

"I don't know. I can try."

"What are you talking about?" asked Tamara, perplexed.

After setting the brake, I lowered my seat back clear down into Paul's lap and stretched out. Closing my eyes, I said, "You need to be quiet, so I can relax."

"You're taking a NAP?" Tamara asked incredulously. "At a time like this?"

"He's going to jump out of his body and go look," Roshayne explained, "but you need to be quiet so he can concentrate."

"Out of his body? What—?"

"Shhhhh!"

I said a quick silent prayer. After the previous three days of God punishing me, I still wasn't sure I would ever be able to jump out again. I put my hands on my stomach, interlocking my fingers, and took several deep breaths.

"What's he doing?" whispered Tamara close to Paul's ear. He put his finger to his lips.

In less than a minute, I was out. I could see the three of them hunched over my sleeping body. I had no way of telling them I had been successful, and they didn't dare interrupt to find out.

I turned and moved back to the trees where I thought Tamara had been looking. At first I was hesitant, expecting trouble. Then I remembered that no one could even see me. I scanned the roadside, but didn't find anything.

I had just begun moving into the trees when I heard a screeching of tires and gravel flying from the other side of the block. I moved instantly through the block and watched as an old, beat-up sedan raced down the road toward town. I made a mental note of what it looked like, then moved quickly back to the trees.

After making five or six passes, progressively deeper into the woods, I found her. She was on her stomach, her legs and arms out at odd angles, and appeared to be unconscious. I couldn't see her face. She was dressed in a pair of tight jeans and a light-colored sweatshirt that was stained all over the back and shoulders.

That looks like blood! I thought in sudden panic.

Her purse had been opened and spilled out just a few feet away. I wanted to turn her over and see how serious it was, so I got down real close. She didn't appear to be breathing; but without my body, I was useless to help.

Back to body! I thought.

Grabbing the steering wheel, I pulled myself upright. Everyone jumped back, startled.

"Tammy was right!" I blurted out. "There's a lady on the ground in the trees, and a car just took off!"

They all spoke up at once.

"Is she dead?"

"Did you see the guys?"

"How do you know all that?"

"We better call the police." "What about the lady?"

"Would someone please tell me what's going on here?" demanded Tamara.

"Paul and Rosh can fill you in later," I said. "Right now, I think we'd better call the police. If we go back there and she's dead, they might think we were involved somehow. We don't want to get our fingerprints and footprints all over the place."

"Is she dead?" asked Roshayne.

"She looked pretty dead to me," I answered.

"Omagosh!" Tamara gasped.

"I couldn't very well check her pulse, though."

"Let's find a phone. Quick!" Tamara said.

"There's a Smith's grocery store a couple of blocks from here," Roshayne offered.

Paul cut in, "I think we should hurry and follow the car before they get away. Otherwise, no one will ever find them."

I considered the options. "Tell you what," I said. "You guys go call the police, and I'll jump out again and see if I can find the car. I'll come back as soon as I know something."

"Okay, but hurry," Paul said.

"I will." I started to lean my seat back again.

"Wait!" he yelled. "Trade places with me first."

"Oh, yeah. Good thinking." I stretched out in the back seat with my head on Tamara's lap, knees in the air, and closed my eyes. "Give me a minute," I said, interlocking my fingers.

The way Tamara looked, you would have thought someone had dropped a dead cat in her lap—her eyes and mouth wide open and her hands out in mid-air, afraid to touch anything. She went as stiff as a board.

I wanted to go back and explain what was going on, but I had more important things to do.

I tried thinking myself to the bad guys' car. I guess I had assumed that since I could will myself to people and places, "things" wouldn't be a problem, either. But it didn't work at all; I just kept hovering over my car. I then spent several minutes moving up and down practically every street in town, looking for the big sedan. I wasted quite a bit of time learning how to control my speed and direction. It took a tremendous amount of concentration and mental focus.

At one point, I had an irresistible urge to return to my body, as if something was pulling me back. *NOT YET!* I commanded myself. *I've got to find these guys first!* With great effort of will, I managed to stay put, in spite of the pull the cord was exerting. Gradually the feeling faded, and I was able to concentrate again on my search.

Maybe they headed for the freeway, I reasoned.

Since they had headed in the direction of downtown, I assumed they would probably be going north. I moved down Main Street to the freeway onramp and started tracking the northbound traffic. I was soon able to match the speed of the traffic, then moved ahead faster so I could scan all the cars ahead of me. It was difficult to judge time, being out-of-body, so I was unsure of how much lead they would have had. I passed Spanish Fork and both Springville exits without finding them, and was about to give up and turn back.

Just then, an unexplainable feeling came over me—a dark and evil feeling, like a third-degree guilty conscience. I scanned the cars ahead of me, and was drawn to one like a magnet. The evil emanating from it was so awful that I had a difficult time not turning and fleeing as fast as possible. I did not want to be around such a terrible feeling.

I stayed high in the air, concentrating on the car, and tailed them for what seemed like hours. Two different times I tried to move down closer so I could see their faces and maybe hear them talking. Both times I was overcome with a squeezing, tormenting feeling and had to go back up.

Being new to the valley and never having seen it from the air before, I was very unsure about where we were once we passed Provo. Eventually we left Utah Valley, rounded a point, and came out into the Salt Lake Valley.

It looks like Los Angeles, only smaller, I thought.

After crossing the entire valley, the car finally left the freeway, meandered its way into a remote residential area, and pulled into an open driveway. I stayed way up high until the occupants had left the car and gone into the house. Gradually the evil feelings faded somewhat, and I decided to risk going down for a closer look. The yard was totally gone to weeds, with a half dozen broken-down cars and car parts scattered everywhere. The house itself was old and poorly maintained. I moved slowly down to the roof and felt the evil bouncing back at me again. Mentally clenching my fists and biting my lip, I forced myself straight down into the living room. It had the same junkyard look as the outside, with beer cans and trash littering the floor.

There, I finally got my first look at the would-be murderers, sprawled out in worn-out armchairs, drinking beer and watching TV. One was fat and balding and appeared to be in his forties. The other was tall and had long hair down over his shoulders, and was much younger. Both were dressed in filthy-looking faded, ragged jeans and tattered T-shirts. I forced myself down lower, where I could memorize their faces, and gave them each a pseudo-name for later tracking.

Frank and Joe, I decided.

I wanted to hear them talk, in hopes they would say something about the lady in the trees, but they were glued to the tube. I decided to look around. I moved through two disastrous-looking bedrooms, the old fashioned, badly stained bathroom, and the most disgusting kitchen I had ever seen in my life. There was an unfinished basement and furnace room, which was at least three feet thick with trash and junk from wall to wall. It would have been impossible for anyone to walk around in it.

How can anybody live in such filth and squalor? Finding nothing of particular interest, I moved back to the living room just in time to hear Joe, the fat one, start talking during a commercial.

"I ain't gonna be the one tells The Man we snuffed the broad. He'll kill us, sure."

"How were we supposed to know she'd have a gun in her purse?" Frank shot back. "I told ya a hundred times already. It was self-defense. Pure and simple."

"I already had her gun, and you know it. Ya didn't have to do her," Joe countered. "All we were supposed to do was rough 'er up and find out where she hid the stuff."

"She saw my face, stupid!" yelled Frank. "She tore the mask off, remember? She was a wild animal!" He touched the fresh red scratch marks on his right cheek. "If she'd gone to the cops, she coulda fingered us. I had to do 'er."

They were both quiet for a minute.

"I still ain't gonna be the one tells The Man," Joe said again, barely above a whisper.

For ten or twenty minutes, neither spoke again, so I finally gave up and moved outside. I made a mental note of the house and street numbers, and decided I'd better get back to the car. I was worried about what might have happened to Paul and the girls.

Back to body.

I still had not figured out how to slow down the return, and was snapped back as fast as ever into my body. When I opened my eyes and took a deep breath, I heard Roshayne's voice.

"You're back! Thank goodness. We were beginning to wonder if YOU were dead."

I sat up and looked around. "Where am I?" I asked.

"In my family room, in case you forgot what it looks like already. My parents are out for the evening."

"I only saw your bedroom the last time I was here, remember?"

Tamara gave me a questioning look. "Her bedroom?"

"I'll explain later," Roshayne told her.

"What took you so long?" asked Paul. He had almost worn out the carpet where he was pacing the floor.

"I followed those guys clear past Salt Lake someplace," I answered. "I never thought freeway speeds would seem so slow. I felt like I was in molasses, and it was really hard to stay focused."

I briefed them on everything I'd seen and heard, which really wasn't much when all was said and done.

"We should tell the police right away," Tamara said when I had finished.

"I agree," nodded Roshayne.

"Tell them what?" asked Paul. "That Bart followed them for ninety miles, floating along at five hundred feet in the air, and then dropped down invisible through their roof to case the joint and eavesdrop? Are you crazy?"

"I still don't understand all this ghosty stuff," Tamara said.

I sniffed at the air and made a sour face. "Holy cow! What's that horrible smell?"

"It's you," answered Roshayne sheepishly, studying her fingernails. "We . . . uh . . . had to put you in a garbage dumpster for a while."

"In a WHAT?" I asked. I jumped up, looking down at my clothes. I tore off my jacket, letting it drop in the middle of the floor. My pants were soaked and stained, and my shoes were a disaster. "Why in the world did you put me in a dumpster? What happened?"

"We've had a pretty interesting night, Bart," Paul said. "We—"

"Wait!" I interrupted. "Tell me about it on the way home. I've got to get to a shower before I die."

"What about Tammy?" Roshayne asked. "Can you take her home first?"

"Okay, but hurry."

We said goodnight to Roshayne. After dropping Tamara off at her house, Paul brought me up to speed on their action-packed evening.

"I called 911 from a pay phone at Smith's, and they insisted that we go back and talk to the police. We were worried that if you didn't come back in your body right away, they would think you were drunk or dead or something. Imagine us explaining that. We had to hide you pretty fast."

"Yeah, but . . . in a garbage bin?"

"It was the only thing available at the time," he said sheepishly.

"Why didn't you just stick me in the trunk or something?"

"We were afraid that the cops might find you there—which they would have. They searched the car thoroughly."

"Why?"

"They thought we might have had something to do with the murder. We were frisked and everything. Then we were locked in the backs of separate police cars and interrogated to death."

"You're kidding. What did you tell them?"

"Just that Tammy had seen them fighting in the woods, and we hurried and called the cops."

"So what about—"

"Nothing about you, don't worry," he said reassuringly. "After they finally let us go, we dashed back behind Smith's to get you, and took you to Roshayne's house."

We rode in silence for a few minutes while I pondered what Paul had told me.

"So she WAS dead," I said as we finally pulled into Paul's driveway. "Any idea who she was?"

"Not a clue. The police wouldn't tell us anything. Said they have to contact the family first," he answered. "This is getting a little scary, Bart."

"I know. But there's nothing else we can do tonight. Maybe tomorrow we can think straighter and figure out what we should do," I said. "We're going to have to figure out a way to let the cops know about Frank and Joe."

"Well, good night," Paul said as he climbed out of the car. Poking his head back through the window, he added, "Terrific first date, huh, Bart?"

"What? Oh . . . yeah. Great dance, too, didn't you think?" We laughed. "What's the deal with us and dances, anyway?"

After parking the car in the garage, I made a beeline for the stairs without Mom or Dad seeing me. I showered until all the hot water ran out.

CHAPTER 14

- Announcements -

Saturday morning, I did my best to act normal as I went through the usual routine. I made it halfway through breakfast before Mom discovered my smelly discarded clothes in the trashcan. About the same time, Dad went out to the garage to go somewhere. They attacked me from both sides simultaneously.

"What happened to your clothes?" Mom snapped, holding up my pants and shirt with her fingertips.

"Bart, what did you do last night?" demanded Dad. "The car smells like dead fish!"

There was no escaping it. My Frosted Flakes went soggy as I related to them the terrible events of the previous night. But it wasn't exactly "the truth, the whole truth, and nothing but the truth." Skipping over the out-of-body stuff, I told them I found the lady in the woods, yelled for Paul and the girls to call the police, then ran after the guys' car to try to get a license plate number. That was all sort of true, anyway.

"Dear goodness," Mom said, her hand over her mouth.

"That was a very, very foolish thing to do, young man," Dad reprimanded me. "They could have killed you."

"I know," I said meekly. "It's just . . . well . . . it seemed like the thing to do at the time. It's not every day you find a dead person in the woods, you know, and I . . . I . . ." My voice trailed off as the enormity of what we had seen and done sank in. I really HAD seen a dead person. And, even though I was never in any danger from Frank and Joe, they WERE real killers.

"Oh, my poor baby," Mom said, grabbing me around the shoulders.

"You should have called us," Dad said. "Why didn't you call us?"

"It was all pretty hectic, Dad. We were pretty busy."

"So what did the police say?" asked Dad. "Do they know anything?"

"I don't know. They wouldn't tell us much last night," I answered. "They roughed up Paul and Rosh and Tammy a little before I got back. They thought they might have had something to do with it. But they let us all go after a while. We'll probably have to go to the station today sometime and answer some more questions."

They sat quietly for a moment.

"This is really getting out of hand," Dad finally said. "A kidnapping and a murder in the same week."

"So, what happened to your clothes?" Mom asked again.

"Well,"I stammered, "I . . . uh . . . tripped coming back through the woods and fell head first into a huge compost heap or something. I had to practically swim my way out of it." Lying to my parents was not something I was accustomed to doing, and I didn't much like it. I didn't know if they believed me or not.

I had just finishing shampooing and deodorizing the inside of our car when Paul called.

"Hey, Bart. The police just called, and they want me and the girls to go down to the station for something. Do you want to come with us?" he asked. "The police don't know anything about you, you know."

"I know, but my folks don't know that. I'd better go with you, or they'll wonder why I didn't."

"I was hoping you would," he said, relieved. "If you can pick us all up, I won't have to ask my parents for a ride. You're the only one with a license, you know."

I gulped. "That's right, you don't have yours yet. Didn't the cops ask to see a license last night?"

He was quiet for a second. "I guess they were too busy to think about it," he answered lamely.

Unbelievable, I thought, slapping my forehead with my hand.

There was a nurse waiting for us when we got to the police station. She took some blood and tissue samples from each of the other three. After that, one of the officers asked them a few more questions. Nothing serious—just details. Then we were asked to wait in the front lobby.

"So, what did you guys tell your parents?" I asked them all.

"Well," answered Paul, "pretty much the truth. There really wasn't much choice, was there?"

"Me, too," answered Roshayne. Tamara nodded.

"Yeah, but what did you tell them about ME?" I asked nervously.

Tamara answered, "My parents didn't really know who I was with, except for Paul, so I left it that way."

Roshayne said, "I just used the words 'us' and 'we' a lot, and stayed away from any specifics."

"Same with me," answered Paul.

"Good," I said, relieved. I told them what I'd told my parents, so our stories would be consistent. "This could get to be a bit tricky if we're not careful," I warned.

A lady cop came out to find us and told us we could go home, and they would call again if they needed anything else.

In the car, Paul mentioned that he had been working on an idea for how to tip off the cops about Frank and Joe, and invited us to his house. Once there, he introduced the girls to his laboratory.

"You sleep in here?" asked Roshayne.

"Amazing," Tamara said, taking in the sight.

"So, what do you have?" I asked.

"Well," he began, "I think we need to drop an anonymous tip, but in a way that they won't know it's from us."

"Can't we just call them on the phone?" asked Tamara, "without saying who we are?"

"No. For one thing, they could trace the call. And even if we called from a pay phone someplace, they would still have our voices on tape and could match them up later."

Trace the call, I thought, remembering my two "almost" phone calls. *Boy, I never even thought of that.*

"Then what?" asked Roshayne, "A letter or something?"

"No. Anything we send would have our fingerprints and our handwriting, and traceable paper and ink. All that stuff."

"So . . . ?" I asked.

"So, we use this." He proudly held up what looked to me like a pile of discarded circuit boards, all wired together haphazardly.

"What is it?" I asked.

"A voice synthesizer," he announced proudly. "Made it myself."

"I figured as much."

"What does it do?" asked Roshayne.

"It imitates voices. We record our message on a regular tape, then re-record it through the synthesizer. I can change the voice enough that it will be totally unrecognizable. In fact, I plan on varying it every two or three seconds through a whole range of male and female voices. It'll probably sound pretty weird, but it'll be impossible to trace."

"I don't understand why we just don't go down and tell them in person," Tamara interjected. "What's the point?"

"The point is," I answered, a bit irritated, "there's no logical reason why any of us should know anything about Frank and Joe. If I told them how I found out, they would probably put me in the state mental hospital and throw away the key."

"And," Paul added, "anything else we say would inevitably lead them to think that we're involved somehow, and know more than we're letting on. We don't have much of a choice."

"Except to keep our mouths shut and let the police figure it out on their own," answered Roshayne.

"Yeah, there's always that," I agreed. *That's what I did last time.*

We spent the next hour or so playing with Paul's invention and getting all our thoughts and comments on tape, using all four voices. When we were all satisfied, Paul told us he would condense the whole thing onto another tape and work up the final synthesized version by Sunday.

Amazingly, there was nothing about the murder in the Saturday evening papers, and nothing on TV, either.

The police are sure keeping a tight lid on this thing. Who was that lady, anyway?

Sunday morning's gigantic paper also came without any news, and I was really wondering what was happening.

After church, I watched the news on every TV channel I could find. The story finally broke around six. There were no photographs or any live footage, since the media had not been on the scene at the time—only a brief description of what had happened and some sketchy details.

Payson must be too far away for them to worry about.

The victim's name was still not mentioned, "pending notification of next of kin." To my relief, they didn't mention much about who had found the body—just "some local teenagers." However, they did report that the police had some solid leads and were investigating the incident.

Solid leads?

I called Paul. "Did you call the police?" I asked.

"Yeah, I did. Right after church. I hitched a ride with my sister to Spanish Fork. She had to return something to a friend over there. I walked to a service station and called from their pay phone."

"Great. They ought to be picking them up by now."

"I have some other news," Paul said. "The police called me a few minutes ago. They said they found some flesh under the lady's fingernails and some hair samples on her clothes. They were happy to report that none of them matched mine or Roshayne's or Tamara's samples. We're not suspects anymore."

"Well, the heat's off. I guess there's nothing else we can do."

Monday morning, during homeroom, we were all being our usual rowdy selves when the morning announcements came on over the PA system. We expected the same girl as always to read through the same boring list as always with the same squeaky, annoying voice as always. Instead, all she said was, "Mr. Palmer has an important announcement to make."

That was unusual. The principal never came on unless there was something real important, like for a fire drill, or after some vandalism or something.

"Students and faculty," he said somberly, "we have some unexpected bad news to relay to you this morning."

I had an instant premonition that it had something to do with Friday night.

"It is with deep regret that we have to inform you of a terrible tragedy that occurred to one of our students last week . . ."

I felt the hair on my neck stand on end. *One of our students?!* Most of the kids stopped talking.

"I'm sure some of you have seen it in the news already. Our junior class secretary and junior varsity cheerleader, Tiffany Short . . ."

TIFFANY SHORT?! The name sent shock waves through my whole body.

"... was beaten and ... killed ... Friday night in a wooded area here in town ..."

NO!

There were some gasps and a couple of swearwords from the students in the room, then it became as quiet as a mortuary. We all stared intently at the speaker.

"... The police are investigating, but at this point they don't have a motive or any suspects ..."

I have some suspects! I shouted to myself, angrily. *I know who they are, the dirty rotten scumbags! Why don't they go and get them?*

My mind only half registered the rest of the announcement. "... there will be several police officers here at the school today to talk with her friends, classmates, and teachers ..."

Oh my heck! Not Tiffany! Beautiful, gorgeous Tiffany! It didn't seem real. It was like a bad dream. *I just saw her last Tuesday at her locker,* I remembered. *She said 'Hi' and smiled at me.*

"... Please give them your full cooperation ..."

The image of Tiffany by the locker faded, and the horrible scene I had witnessed in the woods came sharply into focus. *That bloodstained sweatshirt! That blonde hair! Her arms and legs lying there all twisted!*

"... the class schedule for today will continue as usual ..."

The same girl I saw every day, right out there in the hall!

"... students will be excused to talk with the officers, at their request ..."

The whole thing made me physically ill, and I could feel my breakfast rising to my throat. I jumped up, sending my desk crashing, and raced for the sink in the corner. Some of the girls in the room started to cry. Most of the kids were too shocked and numb to say or do anything.

The last thing I heard before running out of the room was, "... if anybody, repeat, ANY ONE of you has ANY information that would assist the police, please come to the principal's office immediately."

I ran down the hall by the cafeteria. Roshayne saw me go past, jumped up from her class, and ran after me. Out in the courtyard,

I slumped down on one of the benches. I was in shock.

Roshayne sat down by me. "Oh, Bart . . ."

Paul soon found us. He looked as if he had been running the fifty-yard dash. "I've been looking all over for you guys," he said, out of breath. "I can't believe it." He sat down hard beside me.

"I can't believe it, either," Roshayne added.

I got up and paced back and forth a few times, then sat back down. "That wasn't just some lady!" I yelled. "It was Tiffany!"

"Why would anyone want to kill Tiffany?" Paul asked. "It doesnt make any sense."

"Maybe it was a case of mistaken identity," offered Roshayne.

"Sure," I said pessimistically. "I just hope the police hurry and pick up Frank and Joe. Maybe I should go find them and see what's going on—"

"Maybe we should let the police do their job," Roshayne said. "We're not going to do any good getting all worked up."

"Okay," I said, trying to calm down. "We've got to relax. We've got to go back to class. We might look suspicious out here."

"The police already know about us, Bart," Paul said. "We're the ones who found her, remember? We just didn't know who she was."

"Tiffany Short," I whispered again in disbelief. "I can't believe she's dead."

"Come on, Bart. Get yourself together, buddy."

"Okay. I'm okay," I said, standing up. I walked around in a small circle and sat back down. "Let's go back," I said, standing right back up again. "Are you okay, Rosh?"

"Yeah," she said, wiping her eyes with the back of her hands. "I'll be all right."

"Let's meet in the auditorium during study time," I suggested. "I need some time to think about this."

After my English class, I went to my locker to put my books away. As I closed the door, I glanced habitually at Tiffany's locker, half expecting her to be there smiling at me. A knot tightened up around my heart as I shuffled slowly down the hall. My throat went dry, and I had a hard time breathing.

I need a drink, I thought, reaching in my pocket for a handful of change.

I had almost reached the pop machine when a thought came to me, out of the blue. *I could look in her locker.*

I had seen her open it dozens of times and had long since memorized her combination. I never really planned on using it, but it gave me a certain satisfaction knowing that I could. I turned and made my way cautiously back toward her locker.

What if someone notices? I worried. I was about to turn around and leave, but curiosity got the better of me. Acting as nonchalant as possible, I spun the dial and lifted the handle. I looked around guiltily to see if anyone was watching, then I opened the door a crack and peeked in.

I sort of knew what to expect. Books, hairbrush, pictures. What I DIDN'T expect was to find it empty. It was totally bare. Completely cleaned out.

As I stood there gaping, the loose change slipped from my hand and rolled around all over the floor. Hurriedly, I knelt down to retrieve the coins. After finding them all, I reached up and grabbed the lower shelf to hoist myself back up. I was halfway up when my eye caught something unusual. Slowly, I knelt back down.

There, underneath the shelf, was a small black book, held in place with two strips of duct tape. I stood up quickly and spun around, scanning the hallway. More nervous than ever, I reached behind my back into the locker and carefully worked the tape loose. Hastily, I stuffed the book in my back pocket, tape and all, slammed the locker shut, and hurried off to the cafeteria.

After lunch, I went back to my locker and was surprised to find a policeman there with the head custodian, opening Tiffany's locker. They were obviously as surprised as I had been to find it empty.

If the police didn't empty it, then who did? I was stumped. *Surely not Tiffany, unless she knew she was going to die.* It didn't make any sense.

Maybe somebody was looking for this book! I thought.

During geometry, I studied the book. It was about three inches by five inches, spiral bound, with about thirty pages. The soft vinyl cover was blank. The first page on the inside read:

#7 - Douglas Fenton

Fenton. Fenton. Where have I heard that name?

The next several pages were filled with all kinds of meaningless mumbo-jumbo. At the bottom of the fourth page was an overly large notation that said:

$3 mil

I knew that "mil" was short for "thousand."

Three thousand dollars, I thought absently.

After about ten pages, the handwriting changed. Up until then, it had been a bold print with a thick black pen. The next several pages were in pencil, and the writing was a flowery cursive. It was largely a repeat of the first section, but rearranged. Still, most of it made no sense at all. *Probably Tiffany's handwriting,* I thought. The bell rang before I could finish.

Paul and Roshayne were both waiting outside the auditorium when I got there. We hurried inside, and I immediately told them about Tiffany's locker and showed them the book.

"What do you make of it?" I asked Paul.

"Pretty strange," he answered as he thumbed through the pages. "It's kind of like an address book, but in code." Roshayne was looking over his shoulder as he turned several pages.

"And why do you think she was hiding it in her locker?" I mused.

"Wait!" Roshayne exclaimed, grabbing the book. "You guys! Look at this!"

There, staring up from the page, in big letters, were the words:

Andrea Fenton - Provo

My face got hot, and my heart started to race. "Andrea!"

"Who's Andrea?" Paul asked.

"She's the girl that was kidnapped last week in Provo!" Roshayne said breathlessly. "That whole story made such a commotion at my house, my mom almost canceled our date last Friday."

Paul stared at the book that he held nervously in his hands. "Yeah," he said. "I heard about that. Her father came up with a ton of money for the ransom, and it was stolen right out of the guy's safe—"

"Wait a minute!" I grabbed the book and flipped back a few pages. "This isn't three thousand dollars. It's three MILLION dollars. Holy cow!"

"Do you think the kidnapping had anything to do with Tiffany's murder?" asked Paul hoarsely. "Whose book is this, anyway?"

"Who knows?" Roshayne answered. "Maybe Tiffany accidentally stumbled onto it somehow and was going to tell the police."

"That would explain what Frank and Joe said about not finding 'the stuff,'" I reminded them. "They were supposed to rough her up to find out where 'the stuff' was."

"I can't see anybody referring to a single little book as 'the stuff,' can you?" asked Paul.

"You mean Tiffany got killed because she had this book?" Roshayne asked in a hushed voice.

"That's the only thing that makes any sense," I replied. "But I can't imagine Frank and Joe masterminding the kidnapping. They didn't look smart enough. Maybe it was 'The Man' they were talking about."

Suddenly it hit me. *Mr. Clawson! He's 'The Man.' Dang! I should have called the police!*

"If they find out WE'VE got this book, WE could be in big trouble, too," Roshayne said.

"Maybe," Paul said. "We just put our own fingerprints all over it, you know."

"Oh, great," I said, exasperated. "Now what do we do?"

"Well, I suggest you keep this hush-hush for the time being," he said, handing it back to me, "until we can figure out what to do with it."

I flipped open to the last page. There in pencil were the words:

Ask Cindy about

"Hey, guys. Look at this."

"Who's Cindy?" Paul asked, reading over my shoulder.

"Must be a friend of Tiffany's," Roshayne said.

"I think we should find this 'Cindy' and talk to her," I suggested. "I'll ask the quarterback boyfriend if he knows her. Rosh, you could talk to the cheerleaders. They're always practicing on the football field after school. Somebody ought to know."

"I think it would be better if I talked with Tom Zeller," Roshayne suggested, "and you talked with the cheerleaders. It would look less suspicious that way."

"You're right," I agreed.

After school, I approached the cheerleaders. They were understandably upset about Tiffany's death, and were pretty rude to me.

Roshayne found me a few minutes later. "Any luck?" she asked.

"All I got was that Cindy was also a cheerleader, and that she and Tiffany were best friends."

"As soon as I mentioned Tiffany's name, Tom told me to 'bug off' and looked like he wanted to hit me," she answered, discouraged. "If I had been a boy, he probably would have."

"I was afraid of that."

"I'll call some girls tonight and see what I can come up with," she offered.

The top story on the news at six was the murder.

" . . . and this just in," said the anchorwoman. "Police have just arrested two men in connection with the murder of seventeen-year-old Tiffany Short of Payson. They have been identified as forty-two-year-old David Frenway of Wichita, Kansas, and thirty-one-year-old Isaac Johnston of Tipton, Indiana. Both men have prior criminal records. No motive has been determined, and it is unknown at this time if they were acting on their own."

Seeing the faces of Joe and Frank on the TV screen gave me an eerie feeling.

"Police raided a house in Rose Park late this afternoon, where the two men were staying, after receiving an unusual anonymous tip by telephone."

Way to go, Paul!

They showed footage of the raid and the aftermath around the house and yard.

"The murder weapon is believed to be a large, blood-stained, Rambo-type knife, which was found in the trunk of their car. Police are also optimistic that the four gouges in Johnston's cheeks will match scrapings of human flesh found under the fingernails of the deceased. We'll have results of those tests, and another update at ten."

CHAPTER 15

- Cindy -

Roshayne called around seven-thirty and excitedly informed me, "I've found Cindy! I just talked to her on the phone!"

"Great!"

"She was suspicious at first, until I told her we were the ones who found Tiffany's body. She wants us to come over to her house right away."

"Hold on." I asked Dad if I could borrow the truck. "I'll pick you up in a couple of minutes. I'm going to call Paul and see if he can come."

It wasn't until we were almost at Cindy's house that we realized exactly where we were.

"This is where we saw Tiffany, you guys!" Roshayne said suddenly.

We were driving past the exact same place, in the exact same direction as we had been the night of the dance. I slowed down, and we looked silently out the right window at the woods.

"I still can't believe we witnessed a murder right here," Paul said.

Cindy's house was around the next corner to the east, about a half a block. She answered the door herself.

"Come on in," she said.

I recognized her from the pep rallies.

"Let's go downstairs to the family room where we can talk," she said, leading the way. We all got settled into the deep couches in front of the fireplace, and Roshayne made the introductions.

"We understand you and Tiffany were good friends," Roshayne said after a brief pause.

"We were like sisters," she replied softly. "We've been best friends since kindergarten. We did everything together."

"I'm very sorry," said Roshayne sympathetically.

"I don't know what I'm going to do without her."

After a moment or two of awkward silence, she looked at us strangely and asked, "Did you guys really see her get . . . killed?"

"Well, sort of," answered Roshayne.

"Tell me what happened."

Roshayne told Cindy about driving by on the way to the dance, and about Tamara seeing the struggle. Paul talked about finding the body, calling the police, and being questioned.

"We really don't know much more than that," Roshayne concluded. "We didn't even know who she was until this morning at school. Mr. Palmer announced it over the PA, and there were cops all over the place."

"So, which one of you found her?" she asked. Roshayne and Paul glanced quickly at me, not knowing what to say.

"I did," I said. I decided it was about time I started telling the truth about what was going on.

Let the chips fall where they may, I thought.

"What . . . did she look like?"

I paused. "I really . . . don't think you want to know the details," I replied.

She nodded her head slightly, then burst into tears. "It's so unfair," she sobbed. "Why did she have to die?"

Roshayne took Cindy's hand in hers and held it tight. Paul and I just looked awkwardly at the floor while she cried herself out.

"I'm so sorry," she said, regaining control somewhat. "I haven't had anyone to talk to since I found out. I've been going crazy here by myself."

"There's nothing to be sorry about," Roshayne assured her. "We understand. It's been a terrible blow for all of us."

After she settled down a little, I decided it was time to get down to business. "Cindy," I said softly, "we need to ask you something." She just nodded. I pulled the black book out of my shirt pocket. "We found your name in this book, and—"

"Aaaahhhhhhhh!!" she screamed, scrambling backwards over the back of the couch. She acted as if I had shown her a live rattlesnake. "Where did you get that?!" she shrieked. "What are you doing with that?!"

She was trembling violently. We were all too surprised to answer.

Her eyes narrowed. "That's what got Tiffany killed!!" she hissed.

Roshayne stood quickly and went around the couch. "We're sorry, Cindy. Honest. We didn't mean to scare you."

"Cindy?" her mom called down the stairs. "Is something wrong, dear?"

"No. No. I'm fine," she replied, struggling to control her voice. "I'm . . . I was just . . . I'm fine, Mom."

I shoved the book back in my pocket as Roshayne led Cindy back around the couch.

After catching her breath, she looked me straight in the eyes. "Where did you get that book?" she asked through clenched teeth.

I explained how I had found it in Tiffany's empty locker that morning. "I didn't mean any harm, believe me," I said.

"They must have broken in and searched her locker," she said, staring at the floor.

"Who's 'they'?" asked Paul. "What's going on here?"

"Maybe if they'd found it, she'd still be alive," she continued.

"Cindy, please tell us what's going on," Roshayne said, grabbing her hands again. "We're only trying to help. We're friends."

Cindy looked Roshayne in the eyes, then leaned back and covered her face with her hands. After several deep breaths, she told us her story.

"Tiff overheard some stuff at her house a while ago. Her dad and his men were planning something that she said sounded real suspicious. She didn't understand it all at first. They talked about doing something with a girl. A couple of days later, she heard about the kidnapping of that girl, Andrea, in Provo, and recognized her name as the same one they'd been talking about in their meeting."

Andrea? Tiffany's dad? That doesn't add up.

Cindy continued. "She wanted to believe that it had been a weird coincidence, but she couldn't get it off her mind. A few days later, the story came out that the ransom had been paid and the girl returned. That same afternoon, Tiff's dad told her and her mom that he'd just been paid a big commission from a business deal. He told them they were going to take a vacation to Europe in a few days to celebrate. He bought her mom a huge diamond necklace and promised Tiffany a new car when they got back.

"Well, she got real suspicious. That was Wednesday, I think. Thursday morning she got up real early, around four o'clock, snuck into her parents' bedroom, and took the keys to her dad's office and desk. In one of the drawers she found that book, along with a whole bunch of other stuff. Six other books just like that one, and some big envelopes."

"The stuff," whispered Paul.

The drawer! I thought.

"She put the key back, then took them all to her room. After she found out what was in them, she got real scared. She didn't dare leave them in her room, so she left real early for school and went to Tom's house instead. That's her boyfriend, Tom Zeller."

"We know," said Roshayne.

"He didn't want to hide anything for her. He's a real jerk, if you ask me. I've told Tiff a hundred times she should get rid of him, but she never listens . . . listened," she corrected herself.

Drawing a deep breath, she continued. "So, anyway, she hid them somewhere else. She wouldn't tell me where." She paused, pointing at my pocket. "Except for that one. That one we studied together all day, trying to figure out all the gobbledygook in there. We didn't understand most of it. One thing's for sure, though. Mr. Clawson was involved somehow with that kidnapping . . . and probably with Tiffany's death."

"Mr. Clawson?" Roshayne asked.

"MR. CLAWSON?!" I shouted, jumping out of my seat.

"Her dad," she answered. "Well, actually, her step dad."

"It WAS him!" I said, staring at the fireplace. *OH MY GOSH! WHY DIDN'T I CALL THE POLICE?*

"Him, who?" asked Roshayne.

I sat back down, then turned to face Cindy. "Why didn't you go to the police?"

"Tiff was hoping somehow that she could persuade him to return the money."

"What was in the rest of the stuff?" Paul asked.

"The other six books had names and numbers and stuff, just

like that one. The envelopes were full of pictures and papers and computer disks. One of the envelopes had some pretty graphic pictures of a man and a lady in a motel room. Another one had a bunch of stuff about some guy stealing lots of money from his company. Anyway, Tiff decided that they were probably being blackmailed. She had a real hard time believing that her step dad could be doing it, but she didn't really feel sorry for the guys he was doing it to. 'They're getting what they deserve,' she kept saying. But Andrea was different. She hadn't done anything wrong. Neither had her father, probably."

"So, what happened?" asked Roshayne. "What did she do?"

"Well, Thursday afternoon, when she went home from school, Mr. Clawson was in a wild rage. Throwing things and swearing. Her mom was terrified and didn't have a clue what was going on. Mr. Clawson's bodyguard, Derek, was also there. And the Indian."

I jumped to my feet again. "Derek! And the Indian!" I shouted without thinking. "I WAS there!"

"Where, Bart?" Roshayne asked. "What are you talking about?"

I was about to remind her of my weird, invisible office visit, then I caught myself. "So, what happened when she got home?" I asked, sitting back down. "Did he know she had taken the stuff?" Roshayne was looking at me funny.

"Not at first. If Tiff had been a little smarter, they wouldn't have suspected. Derek started asking her some pointed questions, and she got real defensive. She ran out of the house and took off. She said she drove around for hours, then went back home real late, like around four in the morning. They were in bed when she got there, and she went really quiet-like to her room. She told me it looked like it had been hit by a tornado. Everything was upside down and thrown around. The drawers had all been emptied in the middle of the floor. Lots of things broken. The mattress had even been cut open. That's when she came to my house."

"No way!" Paul said. "He tossed her room?"

"What did you tell your mom?" Roshayne asked.

"My mom never knew she was here. Tiff knocked on my window, and I hid her in my room. She stayed here all day Friday. I played music real loud after school to cover our talking, and brought her some food to eat."

"What about your brothers and sisters?" Paul asked.

"I'm an only child," she said. "So is . . . was Tiff. That's what made us so alike. She was worried all day that Mr. Clawson would still know where she was . . . because of the Indian."

"The Indian?" I asked, alarmed.

"Tiff said he's a medicine man or something. He does strange things—I don't know. He chants with rattles or something. Tiff said he can see where people are all the time. Like a crystal ball or looking in a fire or something. She was really afraid of him."

His magic!

"Weird," Paul said.

"Anyway, I went to school as usual on Friday. When I got home, Tiff was all curled up in my closet, scared to death. She said she'd called Tom during lunch from my phone. He lives by the school and goes home for lunch. He told her that their house had been broken into sometime before lunch, and the whole place was a big mess. Their furniture was all destroyed. Their china cabinet was broken open and everything—just like Tiff's room. They called the police, but they wrote it off as a burglary. Tom had no idea what was really going on."

"Holy cow!"

"I told Tiffany she needed to run away somewhere. We took a bunch of food from our pantry and some of my clothes, and she was going to take off in the middle of the night. Her car was hidden in the woods across the street where nobody could see it. My parents always go out on Friday, and I had a date. It was the home-coming dance."

"Yeah, we know," whispered Roshayne.

"I didn't think I could cancel without raising suspicions, so I went. When I got home, she . . . she was . . . gone." Cindy started crying again. "I looked everywhere. I decided maybe she got scared and took off early, so after a while I went to bed. I never even knew about the police being right around the corner." She stopped to wipe her tears away. "Saturday morning I found her car still parked in the woods, with the food and clothes in the backseat. I called Tom's house and Tiff's mom. Neither of them had seen her.

"Then Sunday I heard about the murder and I knew . . ."

She cried uncontrollably for several minutes. Roshayne put her arm around her and held her.

"I'm afraid," she sobbed. "I'm afraid they're going to—"

"They're not!" Roshayne said with authority. "Don't worry. You'll be okay."

After she regained control, I asked her, "Cindy, how did Tiffany hear all this stuff? Where was she?"

"She'd been using the phone or something in her dad's office when she heard them unlocking the door. She ran and hid behind the curtain—"

"The curtain?" I blurted out. "A big, blue velvet curtain?"

She nodded.

"In his office?"

She nodded again.

"That's how I got there! SHE was there! I was thinking about Tiffany, and—"

Suddenly I jumped out of my seat like I had been electrocuted. *Someone is watching us!*

I spun around and looked everywhere. Nothing. The others looked at me, puzzled, and Paul stood up. "What's wrong?" he asked. "What's—?"

I cut him off with a quick hand gesture. There WAS someone there. I knew it. I could feel a very evil presence. Quickly I looked down the hall, up the stairs, and behind all the furniture.

"Bart, what are you looking for?" Roshayne asked. "What's wrong?" Cindy's eyes were wide with fright.

"We've got to get out of here!" I said. I grabbed my jacket from the couch and started pulling Cindy to her feet.

"I'm not going anywhere!" she objected. "This is my house!"

The feeling became so strong that I felt like I was choking. "I've got to go!" I bounded up the stairs, three steps at a time, and rushed outside. As soon as I got out the feeling subsided, and I ran to the truck.

Paul came running right behind me as I climbed behind the wheel. "What in the heck's going on, Bart?" he demanded. "Are you losing your mind?"

Roshayne was saying a hasty goodbye and apologizing to Cindy at the door.

"Get in," I ordered. "Come on, Rosh!"

She came running, and they both jumped in the truck. I took off, leaving tire marks on the driveway. For several minutes they just stared at me. Out on the highway, I slowed down a little.

"What in heaven's name was that all about?" Roshayne finally asked.

"I don't know," I answered. "I panicked."

"You can say that again," Paul said.

"I just felt . . . suffocated all of a sudden."

"Well, it was a pretty rude thing to do, running out like that," Roshayne said.

"I know," I said. "I'm sorry."

"What's all this stuff about a curtain? And an Indian?" Paul asked.

"I was there, Paul," I answered solemnly. "Out-of-body. The office."

Understanding flooded his face. "Jeez Louise!"

At Roshayne's house, I reached in my pocket and tried to hand her the book.

"What do you want me to do with that?" she asked, drawing away.

"I want you to take it and hide it someplace," I said. "Somehow, I think it'll be safer with you than with me."

"I don't know—"

"Please?" I begged. She grabbed it and ran to the house.

CHAPTER 16

- Jill -

Tuesday was Tiffany's funeral, and school was let out early to allow students to attend. The chapel was filled to overflowing. In the parking lot, I noticed a big Channel Five truck and a man with a mini-cam on his shoulder.

I was surprised at how calm and reverent the whole thing was. The speakers were good and the songs were touching. It was a real emotional gathering.

The burial took place in the Spanish Fork cemetery. I had arranged to use the family car, and took Roshayne, Paul, Tamara, Neil, and Scott with me. I couldn't help thinking that it was the first time we had all been together since the accident. Of course, Jill wasn't there, since she was still in the hospital. I also noticed that as soon as Scott fastened his seat belt, the rest followed his lead without even saying a word.

During the funeral, I had not been able to see Tiffany's family at all. Even at the cemetery, there were so many people that we couldn't get anywhere close.

I did see Cindy and her parents. Cindy cried nonstop. I wanted to talk to her and apologize for running out on her, but I never got the chance. Once the graveside service was over, she left right away with her folks.

We decided to hang around a little and watch the people. Tiffany's mom stayed seated by the casket for a long time, but Mr. Clawson left promptly after the prayer. We circled around the crowd to try to see him, but he made a quick beeline for his limo. I nudged Paul when I saw who was holding the door open for him. "It's Derek. The bodyguard," I whispered.

"He looks like the Incredible Hulk," he observed. "He's huge."

"I sure wouldn't want to run into him in a dark alley," I said. The Indian was nowhere in sight.

As the crowd dispersed and we were headed for my car, Neil grabbed me by the arm and pulled me aside. "Bart, I need to talk to you about something before we leave. Can we go somewhere?"

"Sure. You guys wait by the car," I said to the others. "We'll be right back."

"Let's go over there," Neil said, heading toward a group of trees. He led me over behind the biggest one he could find, where we were pretty much out of sight.

"So, what's up?" I asked.

He looked all around, real nervous. "Bart, I need to ask you a really big favor."

"Okay," I answered hesitantly.

"It's about Jill." He paused. "See, she's still in a coma, and the doctors are starting to get real worried about whether or not she'll ever come out of it. It's been over five weeks now."

"I heard. I'm real sorry, Neil. I know you two were tight. But what can I do?"

"Well," he said, fidgeting. "I heard you can do things. Leave your body and stuff."

My eyes narrowed. "Who told you that?" I asked.

"Tammy said some things. You know . . . about Tiffany's murder Friday night."

Figures, I thought. *I should have told her to keep her mouth shut.*

"So?" he asked. "Can you do that kind of stuff?"

"Neil, listen," I said. "Tammy had no right telling you anything of the kind, you hear? What do you think people would say about me if something like that started getting around the school?"

"I won't tell anybody, I promise. And the only reason Tammy said anything was because she heard me talking about Jill and thought—"

"Thought what?"

"Thought maybe you could talk to her," he blurted out. "I told her it was impossible, but she insisted that I ask you."

"Jill's in a coma, Neil. How am I supposed to talk to her?"

"To her spirit."

"What?"

"Well, she's not dead, so her spirit has to be there somewhere," he reasoned. "I figured . . . well, actually, Tammy figured you might be able to see her spirit and talk to her. I mean, what does the spirit do when you're in a coma, anyway?"

"You've got to be kidding. What makes you think I could do that?"

"I don't know, Bart. I just thought—" he stopped, obviously sorry he had brought it up.

"What would I say to her, anyway? Even if I could?"

Neil started to get even more nervous. "You remember that special youth meeting we had a few weeks ago at church?" he asked.

"Yeah," I nodded. "The speaker gave a really great talk on morality and chastity."

"Yeah, well, he said a couple of things that have really been bothering me, and I'm starting to get really worried."

"About what?"

"He said that if anybody has ever been involved in . . . you know . . . wrong stuff, that you better not die without repenting. He said, 'Don't you dare die. You have no right to die like that.'"

"Neil, what are you saying?"

"Jill and I—"

"Listen," I cut him off. "You don't have to tell me this stuff. I don't want to know."

"Please, Bart," he begged, grabbing my shoulders. "I need you to know. I need your help. Jill and I did some things we shouldn't have done, okay? Nothing real serious, but bad enough. You understand?"

"Okay," I said slowly.

"So, now I'm really worried that she might die and go to . . . you know . . . to the devil! I couldn't live with myself if that happened."

"She's not going to die, Neil. Come on."

"She might, Bart!" he blurted out. "Nobody ever thought Tiffany would die, either," he pointed in the direction of Tiffany's grave, "but she's gone now, isn't she." It wasn't a question.

"Okay," I said. "So what is it you want me to tell her? If I can talk to her, that is."

"I want you to tell her that I'm really, really sorry about what happened. I'm REALLY sorry, Bart. And I'm sorry about the accident, too. If I'd done a better job of driving, all this wouldn't have happened."

"That wasn't your fault, Neil, and you know it," I told him. "The brakes went out. It could have happened to anybody."

"But it didn't happen to anybody, Bart. It happened to ME. And I'm afraid I'm going to have to spend the rest of my life feeling guilty. For both things." Tears were forming in the corners of his eyes. "I just don't know if I could handle that."

"Relax, okay?" I said. "Things will work out. I'll find a way. Don't worry. I'll try during study hall tomorrow."

"Today, Bart. It's got to be today. Please?"

"Okay, okay. I'll lock myself in my room when I get home or something."

"Thanks," he said, heading back toward the cars. "You're a good friend, Bart. I mean it."

"It's nothing."

"Oh, and Bart?" he stopped again.

"Yeah?"

"Tell her I love her, will you?"

The afternoon got too busy for me to get any time to myself, and it was bedtime before I knew it.

I lay down and started thinking about the vibrations, and they came almost instantly—like a subconscious reflex. I let them run for a minute, then slowly lifted myself out of my body, feet first. It was like my toes took over and just peeled the rest of me out upside down. Strange.

After collecting my thoughts and being sure I was out, I concentrated on Jill and immediately headed out the window.

I arrived instantly at Jill's bedside in the Provo hospital. She looked peaceful, lying on her back with her arms at her sides and her head propped up a little. Her face was scarred, but it was healing and didn't look at all like I thought it would. Her hair had been cut really short. There was the barest sign of the scar right at her hairline. She looked for all the world like she was just sleeping, and I half expected her to open her eyes whenever the next nurse walked by.

She had a small, clear tube running to her nose to help her breathe. She also had an I.V. hanging by the bed and running to her left wrist. There must have been other wires and things connected under the sheets, because there was a heart monitor running, beeping with every heartbeat. There were other monitors also, but I didn't know what they were doing. Neil had said something once about watching brain activity or something.

I stood there watching her for several minutes before I finally remembered I was supposed to talk to her.

"Hi, Jill," I said out loud. *"It's me. Bart."*

To my utter surprise, she answered, *"Hi, Bart."* It was Jill's voice, but her mouth never moved.

"You . . . you . . . you know I'm here?" I asked hesitantly, looking down at her still face.

"Of course I do," she answered. *"You're standing right by the bed."*

I was shocked. *"You can see me?"*

Her eyes were obviously closed. She hadn't so much as blinked.

"I can see you plain as day, Bart. Can't you see me?"

"I'm looking right at you, Jill."

"Not at my body," she chuckled. *"Up here. By the ceiling."*

My eyes flew to the ceiling, and there was another Jill, hovering right over my head. Seeing another spirit person for the first time came as a big shock. She looked just the same. I could barely tell the difference. Of course, there were no scars on her face and her hair was long and shiny.

"What's the matter, Bart?" she said. *"You look scared."*

I heard the words, but again her mouth didn't move. It was frozen in a slight smile the whole time.

"I'm not scared—" I started to answer. I realized that I was not using MY mouth, either. I had just formed the words in my mind, and they were immediately transmitted to her. She did the same back to me. Like telepathy.

"I'm not scared," I repeated mentally. *"I just didn't expect to see you up there, that's all. You look beautiful, Jill."*

"Why, thank you, Bart."

Having overcome the initial shock, my curiosity took over, as usual. *"Can I touch you, Jill?"*

"Of course," she answered simply. She reached out, took my

hand, and pulled me up even with her. It felt to me just like holding a physical hand. I took her other hand and held them both for several seconds. It was an awesome feeling, floating up there by the ceiling with another spirit person—nurses walking by and not seeing us or hearing us at all.

"So, what are you doing here, Bart?"

"I came because Neil asked me to," I answered. *"He's worried about you, Jill. He's afraid you're going to die."* I paused. *"Are you . . . are you going to die, Jill?"*

"I sure hope not," she replied. *"I think I just need to heal some more before I can wake up."*

I was relieved. *"Neil is feeling very guilty these days. About causing the accident and all,"* I said.

"There's no reason to be. I know it wasn't his fault."

"I told him the same thing, but he feels bad anyway."

"Tell him it's okay."

I paused, gathering courage for the next part. *"He's also feeling very guilty about . . . about . . ."*

I didn't know how to say it. It was hard enough talking to boys about things like that.

"I know, Bart," she said, sparing me the agony. *"I know. I've been spending a lot of my time here repenting."* She laughed lightly. *"There's not much else to do."* Serious again, she said, *"Please tell Neil not to worry. Tell him to straighten things out with himself, and I'll be fine. He needs to pray, Bart. He hasn't prayed in a long, long time."*

"I'll tell him," I promised.

"Thank you," she said.

After a moment of silence, I said, *"I think I should go now."*

"Okay. Thanks for coming, Bart. It means a lot to me."

"Oh, I almost forgot. Neil said to tell you he loves you, Jill."

"I love him, too."

"See you soon, Jill."

The trip back to body was quick, as usual, but the re-entry was not as violent. It was more like . . . wiggling into a sleeping bag until it fit right. I opened my eyes and stared at the ceiling as the vibrations faded away. Realizing that Neil had probably been agonizing all day, I decided I'd better call him right away. I glanced at my clock as I got up.

I was only out-of-body for seven minutes, I marveled. It seemed much longer.

"Neil? It's Bart."

"Yeah?"

"It was amazing, Neil. I talked with her. I saw her spirit. I even held her hands—her spirit hands. It was just like holding real hands. It was awesome . . . and she was so pretty."

"Gosh," he said.

"She seemed happy, and looked very peaceful," I continued.

"Did you tell her?"

"Yes, I did," I replied. "She said she knows the accident was not your fault, and to quit punishing yourself." Neil remained silent, breathing heavily into the phone.

"She also says she's sorry about the other stuff, and says she has been repenting ever since the accident."

"She has?"

"She wants you to sort out your problems before she wakes up, Neil. And to start praying. I know it won't be easy, but that's what Jill wants you to do."

"I know," he said. "It's just that . . . it's hard, that's all. Is she going to wake up soon, then?"

"As soon as her body heals a little more." We were both quiet for a moment.

"Thanks a bunch, Bart. I owe you."

"You don't owe me anything. What are friends for?"

"Thanks, anyway."

"Oh, Neil?" I remembered at the last minute. "She says she loves you, too."

That did it. The floodgates broke wide open, and he busted out in tears. He hung up clumsily, without saying another word.

CHAPTER 17

- Hostage -

Wednesday and Thursday in school, I watched for Cindy all day in the halls. I figured she must have stayed home again. Thursday, when I was leaving study hall, Roshayne found me.

"What do you think we should do?" she asked. "About Cindy and . . . you know."

"I think we should be as quiet as church mice right now," I answered. "Let's let the police work on it. Maybe Frank and Joe will talk . . . or whatever their names were."

"What about the kidnapping thing?" she persisted.

"That girl's back home and safe already," I responded. "There's no hurry. Let the cops work it out."

I didn't want to let on to Roshayne, but I was afraid of getting any more involved. It was bad enough already that I had found that stupid book.

Friday morning I looked all over for Cindy again, and was starting to get worried about her. During lunch, I went to the office and asked for her schedule. Her next class was history—right near my locker. I waited until everybody was seated, and still didn't find her. Back at the office, I asked the receptionist if she had been absent from school.

She thumbed through some papers, then told me, "Cindy hasn't been here at all since last Friday."

I told Roshayne and Paul at the beginning of study hall.

"She must really be feeling down," Roshayne said. "We should go by after school and see her again."

"Let's go call her right now," I suggested. "We can see how she's doing and make sure it'll be all right to stop over."

Using the pay phone in the front lobby, Roshayne dialed her number. "Hello? . . . is Cindy there, please?" she asked.

After a short pause, she said, "This is Roshayne Pennini. I was at your house visiting Cindy on Monday night with a couple of guys . . . she WHAT?" The color drained from Roshayne's face.

"What is it?" I asked, alarmed.

"When? Where? I can't believe it . . . I'm so sorry," she said softly. "Yes . . . yes, I will . . . I promise . . . okay. Goodbye." She hung up and stood staring at the phone.

"What happened?" I asked anxiously.

"That was Cindy's mom," she answered, bringing herself back to reality. "Their house was broken into during the funeral Tuesday. She said it was turned upside down."

"Oh my heck!" Paul said somberly.

"Cindy was in shock," Roshayne continued. "Her mom said that after she saw the living room, she panicked, jumped in her car, and took off. They haven't seen her since."

"She ran away?" Paul asked.

"Either that, or . . ." She left the rest unsaid.

"You think they found her?" I said. "Holy schmoly!"

"Bart, we've got to do something!" pleaded Roshayne. "She could be in real danger somewhere!"

"She could just as easily be dead already," Paul said.

"Don't say that!" she shouted at him.

"Are the police looking for her?" I asked.

"Yes," she answered. "Her parents filed a missing persons report, but they don't have a clue."

"If it's Tiffany's stepfather and that weight lifter guy, they could have her at his house right now," Paul said. "We should tell the police everything we know."

"Bart!" Roshayne said suddenly, breaking out in a smile. "You can find her!"

"What do you mean, I can find her? I don't have any idea where she is."

"You don't need to. You can use your gift. You know her. You know her name and her voice and what she looks like. All you have to do is go out-of-body and THINK about her, and you'll go there, wherever she is!"

"Yes, of course. Why didn't I think of that?"

"Go right now, Bart," she said, grabbing my shirt and shaking. "She might already be in big trouble. We can't afford to wait another minute."

"Right now?"

"YES! We still have twenty minutes of study hall left! That should be plenty of time!"

"We could hide out in the light room," Paul offered.

"Okay, let's do it."

We made it through the catwalks in record time.

"Are you guys just going to sit here and wait, then?"

"I want to know as soon as possible," Roshayne answered. "The sooner you find out where she is, the sooner we can tell the police and they can go get her."

"Yeah, hurry Bart," Paul said. "We'll wait for you."

I was already thinking about Cindy when the vibrations came, and, as soon as I jumped out, I was on my way.

I came to a stop seconds later, just in time to see Cindy being struck violently on the side of her face. I jumped back in surprise. The blow sent her sprawling onto a small, cot-like bed a few feet away. I recognized her attacker immediately as the bodyguard, Derek. He grabbed her by the arm and pulled her roughly to her feet again.

"If you don't tell me where they are, there's going to be another funeral!"

I was horrified. Cindy's face was black and blue from being struck many times already. Her left eye was swollen half shut, and there was a trickle of blood coming from her left nostril.

"I . . . I don't know," she said in a whimper.

"I think you do!" he yelled in her face, lifting her a couple of feet off the floor.

Cindy hung limply. "I told you, she didn't tell me," she cried. "Please don't hit me."

Derek dropped her back on the bed. He paced back and forth a couple of times, then came back and stood over her threateningly. "Mr. Clawson will be here tomorrow. If your memory doesn't improve by then, I will have no choice." With that, he stormed out the room. I heard the electric click of the door locking behind him.

Cindy remained still on the bed for several seconds before getting up and limping weakly to the adjoining bathroom. As she walked away from me, I noticed a shiny silver stainless steel collar around her neck, attached to a steel cable about a quarter of an inch thick and four or five feet long. The other end of the cable had a loop in the end, which was sliding along a larger cable. It was strung from the far wall of the bedroom, through the open doorway and into the bathroom over the sink. *She's being kept like a dog on a dog run.*

The only furniture in the room was the bed and a small end table, which was covered with dirty dishes. The bathroom had an old-fashioned bathtub, the toilet, and a freestanding sink. I couldn't see a mirror or any of the usual bathroom articles.

After washing her face, Cindy returned to the bedroom and lay carefully down on the bed. She covered her eyes with the palms of her hands and began to cry. I stood over her and tried desperately to talk to her.

"Cindy, it's me, Bart." It was no use. She neither saw nor heard. *I've got to do something. I've got to get her out of here.*

There was a small window high up on one wall, which led me to think we were in a basement. The window had been covered over with a thick piece of metal welded in place. The bathroom had no other doors or windows. The only way out was the heavy metal door that Derek had used, which had no doorknob at all on the inside.

The one unusual thing about the room was the mirror above the bed, which appeared to be built into the wall and was very thick. I moved through the bedroom wall and found myself in a nicely decorated family room, with a pot-bellied stove and heavy leather furniture. The mirror in the wall was actually a one-way mirror through which Cindy's captors could watch her at will. Moving around to the door, I discovered that it was controlled and opened by a sophisticated-looking electronic keypad.

If I could see Derek open this door, I could learn the code.

I heard him moving around upstairs, but realized it could be hours before he came down again. *I can't wait around all afternoon,* I decided. *I need to find out where we are. I don't even know what city I'm in.*

I was about to move upstairs and outside, when I felt strongly that I needed to return to my body. It felt just the way I had felt while tracking Frank and Joe, which we had determined to be about the time my body had been dumped in the dumpster.

Something must be wrong. I've got to get back.

When I opened my eyes, I could feel my whole body being rocked violently by the vibrations, more than I had ever felt them before. Then I realized it was not the vibrations at all, but Roshayne and Paul shaking me as hard as they could.

"Get up, Bart!" Roshayne was whispering loudly right into my ear. "Hurry up!"

I sat up just as the door to the light room opened and two of my tech crew friends walked in. They stopped in surprise.

"Hi, guys," I said as nonchalantly as I could.

"What are you guys doing up here?" one of them asked, a little flustered. "We didn't expect anybody to be here."

"Same as you, probably," I answered. "What time is it?"

"You're late for your last class, if that's what you're wondering," he answered.

"Shoot!" I said, feigning ignorance. "We'd better hurry." The three of us stood and left quickly, running through the catwalks as fast as we could.

Once in the hall, I asked, "Where did THEY come from?"

"We saw them come into the auditorium and watched them walking around on the stage for several minutes," answered Roshayne, "but we weren't too worried until we saw them climbing the stairs. We were afraid we weren't going to be able to wake you up before they got there. That would have been difficult to explain."

"So, what did you find out?" asked Paul. "Did you find her?"

I stopped walking. "Yes, I found her, and she's in real big trouble." I related to them everything I had seen.

"Let's call the police right away!" exclaimed Roshayne, heading for the lobby.

I grabbed her arm and stopped her. "We can't, Rosh. I don't know where she is. I didn't have a chance to get outside."

"Then hurry and go back!" she urged.

"From where?" I asked. "Right here in the hall? Besides, I don't think calling the police is going to be such a good idea."

"Why not? We can't just leave her there," she protested.

"I don't intend to," I countered, "but if we knew where she was and called the police, do you know what they would do? They'd storm the place with their SWAT team and probably get Cindy killed. From what I've seen, I don't think Derek would negotiate for a second with the cops. He'd shoot her and go out with guns blazing."

"But you said he was going to kill her anyway . . . tomorrow morning!" Paul said frantically.

"We're going to get her out ourselves," I announced.

"WHAT?" they both replied.

"I can do something the police can't. I can go inside without being seen."

I led them to a bench in the lobby and outlined my plan.

CHAPTER 18

- *Surveillance* -

The first step was to find out where Cindy was being held, and I couldn't do that until bedtime. As soon as I could, I jumped out and flew out of the house.

When I stopped, I realized that I was not in Cindy's room. I was at Roshayne's again.

For Pete's sake. I wasn't even thinking about her . . . was I?

I decided to hang around for a minute. *It's not like I came on purpose,* I rationalized. *And I never really promised that I wouldn't, anyway.*

Her room was exactly the same as I had seen it the time before—neat and tidy. Roshayne was sleeping on her side and looked absolutely radiant.

"I'm sure sorry I got you in the middle of this," I said to her.

Paul and I had given her the option of not going with us on our rescue mission, but she had insisted. I knew she was scared, all the same.

I moved around to the other side of the bed, where I could see her face better. It was half covered by her hair, and it was too dark to see her features clearly. *Sure wish it was lighter in here,* I thought.

Just like that, it was lighter. I wasn't sure how I did it, but it seemed that the light was coming from me.

That's better, I congratulated myself. Then I said, "You sure are beautiful, Roshayne Pennini."

To my surprise, her eyes flew wide open. She bolted upright in bed and slammed back against the headboard. She looked right at me and was on the verge of screaming when she finally recognized me. Her eyebrows furrowed deeply.

"Bart! What are you doing here?" she demanded in a hoarse whisper. She glanced quickly at the door on one side and the window on the other. "How did you get in?" Before I could answer, her eyes went wide open again. "My gosh, Bart. You're as white as a ghost. There's light coming from all over you!" Her eyes went wider still as she looked down at my feet. "My gosh! You're floating in the air!" Realization sank in. "You're a spirit!"

"You can SEE me?" I asked, stunned. "And HEAR me?"

"Of course I can," she answered. "I'm talking to you, aren't I?" Her expression changed again to something between angry and suspicious. She folded her arms. "Bartholomew Elderberry!" She sounded like my mother when I was in trouble. "Why are you spying on me? How many times have you been here in my room?!" She sat straight up, putting her fists on her hips. "You pervert!! Get out of here this instant!!"

"I'm not spying on you, Rosh. I promise. This is only the second time. I was trying to go to Cindy and just got sidetracked somehow."

"Sidetracked," she repeated, still glaring at me.

"I promise. Scout's honor. Cross my heart and hope to die." I made an imaginary 'X' on my chest.

She studied me for a minute. "What did you say?"

"I said, 'Cross my heart and hope—'"

"No, not that. When you woke me up. What did you say?"

"I said . . ." I replayed the events in my head. "I said . . . you're beautiful," I answered shyly.

"Do you really think so?" Her eyelashes started fluttering like butterfly wings. She settled back against the headboard and blushed. It was incredible how she could change emotions so fast. I was struggling for something to say when she shot up in bed again.

"Bart! Do you realize what this means?!" Her eyes were almost exploding.

"What?" I choked out.

"Bart, you can show yourself to people and talk to them while you're out! I can see you and hear you! Don't you realize what this means?"

"Well, I—"

"How did you do it?" she asked, suddenly pensive.

"I . . . I don't know. It was dark, and I wanted it to be a little lighter, I guess."

"This is SO neat!" she responded excitedly. "All you have to do is think something, and you can do it! You could probably do just about anything you wanted, Bart. Like Superman!"

"Well, not anything," I replied, glancing down at her covers. "I don't have X-ray vision." She instinctively pulled her covers up over her chest. "Yet," I added with a grin.

"Bart! Get out of here!" she teased, blushing deep red.

"Okay, I'm going already. I'll see you in the morning. Early," I reminded her.

I thought "darkness" and "invisible," and the room became dark again. I stayed there another minute or two until I was sure that she could no longer see me. She lay back down and stared dreamily at the ceiling with a cute little smile on her face. I'm sure she thought I was gone, or she would never have said the words.

"I love you, Bart," she whispered softly.

Wow!

Cindy, I thought.

Seconds later, I was standing in the small room by her bed. It was late in the evening and she was already sleeping, curled up in a ball. I hadn't noticed before that there were no bedcovers. Just a thin, old-looking mattress. She looked cold and miserable. The lights were out and the room was dark, except for a small nightlight that seemed to be built into the bathroom wall. The rest of the electrical fixtures, plugs, and switches had all been removed and covered over. I shuddered to realize that she had been a prisoner in that dark cell for over three days already.

I moved upstairs, straight up through the ceiling, and found Derek sprawled out in the living room, watching TV. He was cleaning a gun, which he had broken down into several pieces in his lap. There were three other guns sitting on the coffee table, between the pop cans and pizza containers.

I went outside, memorized the house number, and moved to the corner to find the street number. Then I proceeded on into town until I could determine where I was. It turned out to be downtown Provo.

Having established where I was, I returned to Cindy's bedside. I concentrated on making myself visible again and saw the room light up immediately.

"Cindy!" I called loudly. She didn't move. "Cindy, wake up!" Her eyes blinked several times, then opened halfway. "Cindy, it's me, Bart. Remember?"

She rubbed her eyes and squinted in the glow of the light. "Who?" she asked, still half asleep.

"Bart Elderberry. I was at your house on Monday night with a couple of friends. Remember? The book?" I said, to jog her memory.

At the mention of the book, she came fully awake and backed up on the bed as far as her collar and cable would allow. "What do you want?" she asked, fear in her eyes.

"Don't be scared. I just came to ask you some questions," I said. "My friends and I are going to come and get you out of here tomorrow."

She was studying me up and down. "Are you . . . a dream?" she asked.

I hesitated. I didn't have time to launch into a full explanation. "You could say that," I conceded. "I'm sort of . . . projecting myself into your consciousness. It's a trick I learned."

"Oh," she said, rubbing her eyes.

"I need to know a couple of things, Cindy. Can you answer some questions?"

"Okay," she said, looking sleepy again.

"I need to know when Derek comes to bring you breakfast."

She was quiet and still for a minute, and I thought she was going to fall asleep again.

"I don't know," she answered finally. "It's light outside when he comes, because I can see a little light around the cracks in the window. He brings me a new tray and takes the dirty ones away." She pointed to the pile on the end table.

I noticed that he was bringing her the meals on paper plates with plastic cups, spoons, and forks. Even the tray was only cheap cardboard.

Pretty paranoid, isn't he, I thought. "Good," I answered out loud. "Does he come any other time?"

"He comes in and beats me sometimes. He thinks I know where Tiffany hid the books."

"Does he know we have one of them?" I asked.

"No. I've never told him anything about you guys."

What a relief. "Okay. Do you know if he ever leaves the house?"

"He usually goes out right after he brings me breakfast, but not for very long. Then sometimes during the day at different times. Nothing regular. I can hear the alarm beep when he leaves and comes back."

"There's a security system?"

"Yes," she answered. She was getting tired and having a hard time sitting up. She looked very weak. "I think they're going to kill me soon," she said absently.

"No they won't, Cindy. Don't worry. We'll come and get you first," I said with conviction. "I'm going to leave you now. Watch me closely. I'm going to just sort of fade away, like a dream. Then you can lie back down and finish sleeping. We'll be here to get you tomorrow morning."

I thought "darkness" again and the light in the room faded away. She watched until the light was gone, then lay back on the bed and curled up in a tight ball again, falling asleep almost instantly.

My next order of business was to find the security system. It was easier than I thought it would be. I wasn't sure what sensors were where, but there were electronic keypads mounted by the front and back doors.

Thank goodness, I thought. If it had been key activated, it would have been impossible to shut down.

With my surveillance done for the night, I returned home to my body.

CHAPTER 19

- Stakeout -

My alarm went off at five-thirty, and I shot out of bed like I was spring loaded. I was dressed and out of the house in ten minutes without bothering to have breakfast. I threw my backpack over my shoulders and pedaled my bike hard to Paul's house. I was just about frozen by the time I got there, having neglected to take any gloves or earmuffs.

I had told my parents we were going to be doing a special project and needed to be gone most of the day. I knew better than to try to borrow the family car again, and the truck wasn't well suited for what we wanted to do. Paul had offered the use of his brother's old "Fun-Van," an older-than-the-hills Dodge van that his older brother had used before leaving home. It was painted psyche-delic orange, yellow, pink, and purple and had been outfitted with a small refrigerator, a sink, four swivel captain's chairs, and a bed in the back. It was perfect.

We picked up Roshayne at around six o'clock and hit the freeway. Paul brought along his toolbox, and Roshayne brought a box full of sweet rolls and a big thermos of hot chocolate. On the way over, I filled Paul in on our discoveries from the previous evening. He was duly impressed.

We got off at the Provo Center Street exit and worked our way into the right neighborhood. The "jail," as we were referring to it, was on the end of a dead-end street and backed up right against the freeway. There were lots of trees and bushes lining the property and all up and down the street. We parked the van against a row of tall hedges about five houses down. We felt about as inconspicuous as a neon sign.

"Time to go to work," I told them. Paul and Roshayne took their places in the middle seats, where they could see the house through the front windshield without being too visible themselves. All the other windows of the van were tinted and covered with curtains. I ate a donut and took my place on the bed.

"You know, this isn't fair at all," Roshayne teased as I got comfortable. "You get to sleep while we do all the work."

I jumped out-of-body and floated slowly into the house. Cindy and Derek were still sleeping. I worked my way through each room, memorizing the layout of the house. I paid particular attention to the front and rear doors and the backyard. Minutes later, I was sitting up on the bed again.

"Okay, here's what it looks like," I said. I drew them a rough sketch of the house, upstairs and down.

"The backyard is very secluded," I told them. "That'll be the best way to get in. You're going to have to break the window on the door in order to turn the dead bolt and the doorknob from the inside. We'll just have to risk the noise."

Paul fished out a crescent wrench from his toolbox and wrapped it with a towel from under the sink.

"There's an alarm keypad right inside the door," I said. "As soon as Derek leaves, I'll come back and give you the code. Plus the code for Cindy's door." He nodded. "You're both going to need to go in. Cindy will need help to get out fast."

Roshayne looked nervous, but nodded in agreement. She was originally just going to stay in the van as lookout.

"After I give you the codes, I'm going to follow Derek. If I see him heading back, I'll come straight back and warn you."

"Are we supposed to wait for you?" Roshayne asked.

"No. Get out of here as fast as possible and hit the freeway. I'll find you, no matter where you are."

"How do we get Cindy loose?" Roshayne asked.

"I haven't been able to come up with anything except the hacksaw idea we talked about yesterday. You'll just have to cut through the cable."

Paul pulled a hacksaw out of his box. "I put in a new blade last night," he said, "and I'll carry a spare. I should be able to get through that cable in under five minutes."

"Cut it right through the loop, where it connects to the collar," I suggested. "That way, we won't have to worry about any cable hanging around." He nodded. "She'll just have to wear the collar until somebody can figure out how to get it off."

"Why don't we pull the van in the neighbor's driveway after he leaves," Paul suggested. "That way we can get to it quicker and leave faster."

"Good idea," I agreed. "And Rosh, make sure you hold the bedroom door open while Paul cuts the cable. Otherwise you could all three end up locked in."

We sat quietly for a long while, watching the house and eating donuts. After what seemed like hours, a light finally came on upstairs.

"I'm going back in," I said as I headed for the bed. "It'll probably take a while for him to get ready and do breakfast and everything, but be ready."

After jumping out, I moved to the house and spent a long time waiting while Derek went through the motions of dressing, shaving, etc. Then he cooked up a huge breakfast of scrambled eggs, sausage, and toast—every bite of which he heartily devoured. After he was satisfied, he cooked some lumpy oatmeal and dumped it in a paper bowl for Cindy.

No wonder she's so weak, if that's all they've been feeding her.

He grabbed a small, school-lunch size carton of milk and headed downstairs. I followed him like a shadow and watched intently over his shoulder as he worked the keypad, memorizing the sequence.

Five, four, five, two, then the green button. I repeated it to myself several times.

Derek pushed the door open, put the breakfast on the table, and shook Cindy roughly to wake her up. I went back to body.

"Five, four, five, two, green button!" I shouted as I sat up.

They both jumped at the sound of my voice, then Paul grabbed the notepad and started writing. "You'd better bring this in with us," he indicated to Roshayne, handing her the pad.

"After you do the code, the door will buzz and you can just push it open." I lay back down without waiting for a response and went into the house for the third time.

Derek had Cindy on her feet and was giving her the third degree again. "Mr. Clawson is a very unhappy man, Cindy," he said, shaking her violently. "I suggest you improve your memory quickly before he gets here, or it's all over for you." He pushed her back down on the bed. "Hurry and eat," he ordered, walking to the door.

He picked up the dirty pile from the table and turned around again, facing her from the doorway. "And wash up a little. You stink. We don't want to make a bad impression, do we?" He kicked up the doorstop and the door swung closed behind him with a heavy click.

Creep!

Derek took his sweet time doing mostly nothing for several more minutes. I debated appearing to Cindy to let her know we were there, but worried that Derek might come down and see me through the one-way mirror. It was nearly nine on the kitchen clock when he finally grabbed his jacket and headed for the back door.

Showtime. I moved in real close again to watch. He unlocked the door, then punched in the alarm code on the keypad to activate the system.

One, nine, nine, one, and the button marked "Away." A sensor in the house somewhere chirped quickly four times. Derek listened, then opened the door and walked out. After shutting the door, he locked both the knob and the dead bolt and headed for his convertible. I rushed back to body.

Paul and Roshayne were kneeling on the floor behind the seats, watching Derek get into his car. I sat up.

"Okay," I announced.

"Jeez, Bart!" Paul cussed, spinning around. "Do you have to scare us to death every time you sit up?"

"Sorry," I said. "Write this down. Hurry." Roshayne had the pad and pencil in her hand already. Paul's tools were sitting by the side door and the engine was running. "The code to leave was one, nine, nine, one. Then he pushed a button marked 'Away.' There's another button marked 'Off.' Hopefully the same code will work with the 'Off' button to shut it down."

"Got it." She scribbled the instructions on the paper.

"As soon as his car rounds the corner, count to five and move in," I said. "I'm out of here."

I was out and hovering at the side of the van by the time Derek drove by. I tailed him from about thirty feet up and thirty feet behind. He drove slowly through several intersections, turned right on a larger street, then drove a few more blocks to an Albertson's grocery store. *I hope he has a long shopping list,* I thought.

Derek meandered aimlessly up and down several of the aisles, picking up a few things here and there and putting them in his cart. I tried to gauge the time I'd been away by what he had been doing, and estimated approximately twelve to fifteen minutes when he pushed his cart to the front to pay.

Not already! I thought in a panic. I waited for him to return to his car and saw him heading back in the direction of the house. *He's going back! I've got to warn Paul and Roshayne!* I took off in a blur, hoping fervently that I would find them in the van.

No such luck.

I stopped in Cindy's room again. The three of them were standing side by side under the darkened window. The cable was dangling loose from the overhead line. I was about to materialize and tell them to hurry when I realized they were frozen in place, staring right through me toward the door.

I turned around and found myself nose to barrel with the biggest gun I had ever seen in my life.

Ahhhhh! I yelled and jumped out of the way.

Mr. Clawson and the Indian were standing just inside the door. Silver Hawk had the hacksaw and the notepad in his hands, studying them. Mr. Clawson was holding the gun and doing the talking.

"Well, well, well. What have we here?" he said sarcastically. "How nice of you to drop in. How did you find us?" Nobody answered. "How did you get in here!?" he demanded. Silver Hawk handed him the notepad, and Mr. Clawson looked at it briefly. His face turned red with anger.

"Where did you get these codes?" he snapped, stepping over to Paul. "Answer me!" Paul stood his ground and said nothing. Without warning, Mr. Clawson swung his arm and pistol-whipped Paul sharply across the right cheek. His face erupted in blood as he fell to the floor. Roshayne bent down to help him. Silver Hawk rushed over, pushed Roshayne to the bed, and yanked Paul roughly to his feet, holding him from behind.

"I asked you a question!" he shouted in Paul's face. "How did you get these codes?" Paul was holding his cheek with his right hand, blood seeping through his fingers. Mr. Clawson swung again, this time from the opposite direction, and caught Paul on the left side just below the eye. He stumbled again, but was held in place by Silver Hawk.

"No! Please!" Roshayne cried, jumping up in front of Paul. "I'll tell you everything! Don't hit him again! Please!"

Mr. Clawson turned his gun on her.

"Wait!" yelled Silver Hawk. He stepped forward quickly, pushing Paul aside and holding his hand in the air. "Wait!" He looked around the room at the tops of the walls, as if searching for something.

"What is it?" asked Mr. Clawson.

"Shhh," he responded, his hand still in the air. Everyone went quiet. Slowly he rotated in place, scanning the entire room back to where he started. After another quarter turn he stopped, looking right at me.

I was shocked. *He knows I'm here!* I moved a few feet to the left, to see if his eyes would follow. They did, but not exactly. I wasn't visible to him, but he still knew I was there. Somehow he knew!

Abruptly, he bolted for the door and ran out of the room. I followed right behind and watched as he threw himself onto the couch. He closed his eyes and crossed his wrists over his chest.

I don't like the looks of this! I moved away behind his head.

In a matter of seconds, he was sitting up again—only he really wasn't! His body was still lying on the couch! As his spirit head came off the pillow, my mind went into overdrive.

He's jumping out! I can't believe it! He's going out-of-body!

Hawk's spirit body rapidly approached the upright position. *He's going to see me!* His head started to turn in my direction.

I can't let him see me! BACK TO BODY! I screamed to myself— just a fraction of a second before his eyes came around.

I sat up on the bed in the back of the van and immediately broke out in a cold sweat. Looking out the window, I saw that I was in a driveway only two houses away from the "jail." Derek's convertible was just pulling into the driveway, and there was a huge black Cadillac parked in front of him.

Derek climbed over his car door, pulled two full bags of groceries from behind his seat, and walked to the house. As soon as he was out of sight, I threw myself into the driver's seat. The van's engine was still running, ready for a quick getaway, so I slammed it into gear and pealed out. I frantically zigzagged my way at top speed through several blocks of residential area before I finally got a hold of myself.

What am I going to do? I've got to think! I pulled into a church parking lot and stopped under a big tree. *If I go back, they'll lock me up with the others, and we'll never get out.* I didn't think they'd seen the van leave, and chances were they hadn't noticed it when they drove in. *If I don't go back, they could kill them!*

I drummed the steering wheel with my fingers, trying to make a decision. I didn't dare go back spiritually, for fear Silver Hawk would see me. *I'll stay here for a few minutes, then drive past and see what they're doing,* I decided. I set my stopwatch for ten minutes and tried to relax.

By the time it got to six, I couldn't stand it any longer. I pulled cautiously out of the parking lot and worked my way back to the house. Trying to be as casual as possible, I cruised by the end of the street.

They're gone! Neither the Cadillac nor the convertible were anywhere to be seen. I stepped on the gas a little and nervously watched the rearview mirror. *Where did they go?* I asked myself. *Did they take the guys with them? Or leave them locked up?*

After a few more haphazard turns to make sure I didn't have anyone following me, I drove downtown and parked in the most crowded part of the Albertson's parking lot. Turning off the engine, but leaving the keys in place, I went back and lay on the bed.

After leaving my body, I forced myself to move slowly and cautiously back toward the house. It took great willpower and concentration NOT to think of Paul or Roshayne or Cindy. I didn't want to instantly show up where Silver Hawk might be waiting. As I moved down the street toward the front of the house, I paid particular attention to whether or not I could feel any evil presence in the area. After assuring myself that I was alone, in the out-of-body sense, I moved into the house and down through the floor into the far corner bedroom.

Slowly, I pushed my head out through the wall into the hallway. Nobody in sight. The door to the "jail" bedroom was closed. I moved carefully forward, listening and watching for any signs of danger. At the door, I stopped and listened again. I could hear some muffled sounds coming from inside. Instead of going straight in, I went around into the family room to the window. I saw Paul and Roshayne bound and gagged, sitting on the floor with their backs against the wall, knees in the air. Cindy was on the bed and appeared to be tied down. Still no sign of Mr. Clawson or Derek or Silver Hawk.

I decided to risk it, and went in. Hovering in the center of the room, I commanded myself to become light and visible. As soon as she saw me, Roshayne started shaking her head violently and making garbled noises through the gag. Her eyes were wide with fright. I couldn't tell what she was trying to say. I looked around in all directions to see if I was being watched, and saw no one.

I was just about to open my mouth and ask her what the problem was, when the lights went out.

CHAPTER 20

- Hawk -

I was struck suddenly from behind with the force of a Mack truck at freeway speeds, and was propelled through the wall and out into total darkness. It didn't occur to me at the time that I was actually underground. All I knew was that I had been attacked by something or someone and could feel a vicious and evil presence all around me. I sensed instinctively that the "thing" intended to "kill" me or get rid of me somehow.

A violent struggle took place; it was like trying to fight off a wild animal. It was ferocious—silent—fast. At first I just tried to defend myself, but the "thing" seemed to know my every thought and move, including all my weaknesses down to the very core of my nerve center, and continually took advantage of them somehow. It attacked and attacked and struck me and pinned me in the most excruciating manner imaginable.

I had never felt such sheer terror. I knew that if I did not fight back, the "thing" was going to win—and I was terrified at what losing might mean.

It seemed that as we fought, we were sinking into a bottomless pit. I fought back with everything I had, but gradually the "thing" wore me down and my mental and spiritual strength slackened. Blackness closed in all around me. Not a visible blackness, but an overpowering and totally consuming feeling of emptiness and utter nothingness.

I was sure that I was about to be cast into outer darkness.

In the midst of my torment, I caught hold of the possibility of prayer.

Help me, God—

"FOOL!" I was cut off sharply by an evil, angry voice, echoing through my entire being and slicing through my consciousness like a two-edged sword.

"YOUR GOD HAS NO POWER! HE WILL NOT HELP YOU NOW! YOU ARE MINE!"

I was too weak to resist further.

"YOU SEE! YOU CANNOT WIN AGAINST ME! I AM TOO POWERFUL!"

It felt as though the very jaws of hell had opened and were ready to swallow me up. Silver Hawk's face suddenly materialized directly in front of me, contorted in anger and vengeance. His eyes were like hot burning fires.

"YOU ARE NOTHING! YOU CANNOT ESCAPE!" he screamed at me.

I prayed again. *Father in heaven, PLEASE help me!*

The thought or inspiration came to me that if I could will myself back to my body, I would be free.

"Yes!" he hissed like a snake. *"Go to your body, boy! GO BACK!"*

I could not understand why he would be giving me up that easy, after fighting so long and hard.

"I KNOW YOU, NOW!!" he seethed. *"YOU CAN NEVER ESCAPE ME AGAIN! WHEREVER YOU GO ON THIS EARTH, I WILL FIND YOU! WHEREVER YOU GO IN THE UNIVERSE, I WILL FIND YOU! YOU ARE MINE, BOY!!"*

In utter despair, I realized that he was right. I would never be able to hide from him as long as he was alive and able to get out of his body.

Suddenly, he released me. Then he pressed his ugly face against mine and shouted, *"GO BACK TO YOUR BODY, BOY!"*

I couldn't stop myself. My mind echoed his command, and the cord snapped me back instantly. I re-entered with the most violent physical jolt I had ever felt, and I tumbled off the bed to the floor of the van. I felt overwhelming relief at being free from Silver Hawk's grasp. Then I became terrified that he had followed me and knew exactly where I was. My suspicions were confirmed as I sensed his evil presence growing all around me, like bad breath.

Quickly, I jumped to the driver's seat and started the van. In sheer desperation, I raced through town and onto the freeway.

As I entered the freeway, the awful feeling left, and I felt he was gone. I continued my frenzied drive, weaving through traffic like it was standing still. Gradually, I let up on the pedal.

I was just reaching the first Springville exit when the feeling returned. He was back!

"You can follow me all you want, jerk!" I yelled angrily into the air. "I know you can't hurt me!" I knew it was a stupid thing to say, but I needed to vent my frustrations. I could almost hear him laughing behind me.

Derek caught up to me just after the second Springville exit and passed me in a blur of black. He pulled in front and forced me to slow down. I tried to pass several times, but he expertly maneuvered me onto the shoulder until I was at a full stop.

I knew it was pointless to try to take off again. Derek leaped from his car and ran to the passenger side of the van, then opened the door and jumped in, holding a gun pointed directly at my head.

"Set the brake and kill the engine," he ordered.

I did.

"Now get in the back."

He pushed me into one of the swivel chairs and was about to throw a rope around me when he noticed the roll of duct tape in Paul's toolbox. He quickly strapped me to the chair, my hands at my side, totally immobilizing me from head to toe. He even strapped my forehead to the headrest and taped my mouth shut.

When he was finished, he dropped into the driver's seat and started the engine. I heard a voice as the right door opened, and recognized it as Mr. Clawson's.

"There's been a change of plans," he said. "Take him directly to the airport. We'll do them in the hangar. There's no time to go back to the house. Hawk will follow in your car."

At the words "do them," my pulse quickened and I had a hard time breathing so fast through my nose. I closed my eyes and forced myself to relax. Derek put the van in gear, and we headed for the Provo airport.

CHAPTER 21

- The Hangar -

I was able to see through the windshield somewhat and watched as we entered the Provo airport compound. We drove past several small planes that stood chained to the asphalt, and past several rows of hangars. Finally, we drove through a large accordion type garage door and came to a stop inside a darkened hangar. Just outside, I could see a twin-prop sitting with its propellers turning at an idle.

Derek cut me loose and hauled me out onto the floor as Silver Hawk pulled up alongside in Derek's convertible. Mr. Clawson was already out of the Cadillac. Paul, Roshayne, and Cindy were pulled roughly from the backseat. We were all herded through a doorway into a dark room and pushed into a pile on the cold floor. Mr. Clawson turned on the light and stood looking down at us. Derek and Silver Hawk tied all of our feet together in one big knot. Derek strapped my hands and arms behind my back with duct tape. The other three were still gagged, with their hands tied behind them with ropes.

"You're the spy," Mr. Clawson said accusingly, staring at me. I stared back. "Take the tape off his mouth," he said to Derek. "I want to talk to him."

Derek ripped the tape off so hard it felt like all the skin went with it, then he and Silver Hawk left the room.

"How long have you been spying on us?" Mr. Clawson asked.

"Long enough," I snapped.

"Are you the local teenagers who called the police about my stepdaughter's untimely death?" he asked. "What did you see?"

"I just saw the guys leave the woods," I replied.

"And then you worked your inner spirit magic and followed them home," he finished for me. "I suppose I owe you for catching them," he said, trying to absolve himself of any involvement.

"Liar! You killed her yourself," I said, getting angry. "You hired those thugs!"

"I didn't do anything of the kind. There is absolutely no way you could possibly link that terrible act to me," he said. "She was my wife's only daughter, and I loved her very much."

"You make me sick," I said with disgust.

"I'm an innocent man," he proclaimed.

"You're as guilty as heck, and I can prove it!" I blurted out.

He looked at me very hard. "You have my books, don't you," he breathed ominously. "I searched her room and her boyfriend's whole house. I was certain that Cindy knew where they were."

"Yes, I have them all," I bluffed, "but you'll never find them. They will be turned over to the police if I disappear, and you will be arrested and convicted of murder and kidnapping and blackmail and a hundred other things!" I spat the words at him.

"Don't make me laugh," he said. "I don't think you're smart enough to set up something like that. Anyway, it doesn't matter anymore. By the time the police see them—IF they see them—I'll be in Mexico. Or Brazil, maybe. My pilot is waiting for me even as we speak."

Silver Hawk came back into the room carrying a five-gallon can of gasoline, and commenced to pour it all over us, and everything in the room. Roshayne and Cindy protested loudly through their gags and tried to wiggle away.

"You're going to kill us?" I asked incredulously. "You're going to set us on fire?"

"I can't just leave all these eyewitnesses around, can I?" he said, sweeping the room with his gun. "Face it. You know too much. You all know too much."

I could see Derek through the doorway, fastening a timing device to a bundle of something. My adrenaline started to race.

"You murderer! You dirty rotten scum!"

"Now, now. Sticks and stones may break my bones . . ." he mocked.

Derek finished his job and carefully set his bundle on the floor, right under Paul's van. Silver Hawk was pouring gas all around and inside of the three automobiles.

"The plane is loaded and ready, Mr. Clawson," Derek said.

Mr. Clawson nodded in his direction. "You have to admit," he said, turning back to me, "it WAS a pretty good setup. Don't you think?"

"What are you talking about?" I questioned, stalling for time.

"Silver Hawk and his magic, of course. He's the ultimate secret agent. You never know he's there. He can follow you to your secret weekly rendezvous with your lover and watch you all night long. He can stand over your shoulder in your office and watch you manipulate bank funds on your computer. He can go in and out of dozens of houses in an entire neighborhood in broad daylight, and never be seen. He can watch you enter your ID and passwords, your account numbers, and your alarm codes." He chuckled. "Of course, you know all about alarm codes, don't you?" he asked, smiling wickedly.

"My favorite trick was the ransom money for that girl, Andrea. It was a stroke of genius, don't you think? Did you read about it in the paper?" he asked. "Hawk worked his magic and followed Fenton all the way from his bank to his house, and then watched him hide the money in his own safe—he saw the combination and the whole works. What a stupid thing to do. That was a much easier place for me to get paid than trying to out-fox the police at some heavily guarded handoff. Although, I'm sure Hawk and I would have worked it out."

"How did you get past the police in their house?"

"The hardware is Derek's department," he replied. "He snuck into the basement and ran a sleeping gas through the heating system. He's the expert with hidden cameras, electronic gadgets, breaking and entering, and the like." He glanced out into the hangar area. "And explosives, I might add."

Derek whispered something in his ear.

"I'm sorry to cut this discussion short," he apologized sarcastically. "I really must be going. I don't suppose I could convince you to come and work for me. The pay is good, and it sure beats getting blown to pieces."

"Stuff it!" I spat back.

"So sorry," he frowned. "Shut the door and set the timer," he barked at Derek. They both stepped out, and the door swung shut with a bang. Seconds later, we heard the engines on the plane rev up and pull away from the hangar.

Immediately we began squirming around, trying to free ourselves, but the ropes were too tight. Then I realized that they had made two mistakes in leaving so fast. One was that they had not taped my mouth.

"Roshayne, let me try to untie your hands with my teeth." She was tied to my immediate right. Cindy was next to her, and Paul was last. I leaned back and tried to get where I could reach the ropes. She started shaking and wiggling like crazy and shook her head at me.

"What?" I said. "What's wrong?" She muttered some things through the gag that I couldn't understand and made all kinds of gestures with her eyes and face.

"Turn your head and let me get your gag off," I said. "I don't know what you're saying." She let out an exasperated grunt, closed her eyes in disgust, and turned her head away from me. It took me several seconds, but I was finally successful in loosening the knot enough that I could pull her gag down over her chin with my teeth.

"Bart!" she yelled in my face. "Jump out! Jump out! You can get help! Go! Go! Go!"

What an idiot I am, I reprimanded myself.

I lay back on my side as best I could, with my feet tied to the others and my arms strapped behind me. I closed my eyes, concentrated on the vibrations, and tried to get out. They came okay, but when I attempted to lift up, I was stopped. It felt as if someone was kneeling on my chest. I tried rolling out the side and out the bottom and was stopped again.

I lifted my eyes and head out of my body a few inches and found Silver Hawk wrapped around me like a net.

"Hello, boy!" he whispered evilly. *"Mr. Clawson has allowed me to come back and watch the sacrifice . . . now that I'm all settled in. I am working my magic from his plane."*

I tried to push him off, and he caused a terrible pain to shoot through me. I remembered the previous fight and knew I was no match.

"Soon, you and your friends will meet the Great Spirit," he hissed.
Making myself physical again, I sat up quickly.

Roshayne asked anxiously, "Did you go already? Did you get
help?"

"I can't get out!" I cried. "Silver Hawk is sitting on me and
holding me in! He won't let me get out of my body!"

"Oh my gosh!" she said, looking nervously around the room.

"Turn around and let me get your hands undone." She turned
quickly. I lay down with my knees in the air so I could get close
enough, and worked the knots desperately with my mouth. My jaw
and teeth ached from the effort, and the taste of gas was nauseating,
but finally the knots fell free. Roshayne immediately leaned over to
untie Cindy's ropes.

"No, Rosh!" I yelled. "My pocket! Reach in my left pocket! I
have a pocketknife!"

That was their second mistake—not searching me. Roshayne
pulled out my scout knife, and in a matter of seconds we had cut
ourselves free. I rushed to the door that led to the hangar and tried
to open it, but it was padlocked securely from the hangar side.
Roshayne tried the same thing with the door leading to the outside.
Same results. Cindy feebly groped along the walls, trying to find
anything or anyplace that would lead to our escape.

I looked at Paul and grimaced. The right side of his face was
covered with dried blood, and his right eye was stuck shut. His left
eye and cheek were so swollen that there was only the barest sliver
of an opening left. He was lying still on the floor, clutching his
chest with both arms.

"We've got to find a way out before the bomb goes off!"
Roshayne screamed. She began pounding on the outside walls with
both fists and yelling at the top of her lungs. "HELP! GET US
OUT OF HERE!" There was no answer.

I examined our prison. The entire room was made of heavy
corrugated metal siding, riveted to steel crossbeams and rafters. The
ceiling was a good twelve feet high and the floor was solid concrete.
The room was bare, except for a large wood desk sitting against one
wall and a few flimsy cardboard boxes with files and papers in them.

"Bart." It was Paul. He was lying still on his back. "Bart, is that
a sprinkler head on the ceiling?"

I looked up at the ceiling. "Yes," I answered.

"If we could get it to come on, we could get ourselves soaked with water. Might help keep us from burning up."

"How are we going to do that?" I asked. "I don't have any matches, and I wouldn't want to light one in here anyway!"

"Don't have to," he mumbled from swollen lips. "Pull the tab."

I knelt down by his side. "What tab, Paul?" I looked around the wall for a fire alarm handle.

"On the sprinkler. There's a metal tab that holds the two little arms open. Pull it out." With Roshayne's help, I pushed the desk to the middle of the floor.

While I was maneuvering, Paul explained, "The metal is soft. When there's a fire, the tab melts. Then the arms fall out and the sprinkler comes on." I climbed up, but couldn't come close to reaching it.

"Too high," I said, discouraged. "We'll have to make a pyramid." I pulled Roshayne and Cindy up with me on the desk. "Cindy, climb up on us." Roshayne and I went down on all fours on the desktop, and Cindy stood carefully on our backs.

"I can't reach it!" she exclaimed. "It's still too high." Stepping back down on the desk, she lost her footing on the wet, gas-soaked wood and toppled to the floor. "My foot!" she screamed. "I sprained my ankle!" She rolled around on the floor in pain.

"I can help!" Paul pleaded. "Help me get up!"

I helped him up on the desk. We stood face to face and locked wrists. Roshayne gingerly stepped onto our arms, and we hoisted her into the air while she steadied herself by holding our heads. She reached.

"I've got it!" she shouted.

There was a loud snap, and we were immediately drenched with water spewing from the pipes. We carefully let ourselves down off the desk as an ear-splitting bell began ringing from somewhere outside the building.

"Get as wet as you can," Paul instructed. "Everywhere you can. It'll help wash out the gas."

As we were standing under the cascading water, we became aware of a new sound coming from outside. We cocked our ears to listen.

"Sirens!" Roshayne shouted. "I can hear sirens!"

We all rushed to the outside wall and began banging as hard as we could.

"HELP!" we yelled in unison. "HELP US!" Every few seconds, we stopped to listen. "HELP!" we yelled again and again. After the seventh or eighth attempt, we heard a voice calling to us from the outside.

"Get us out of here!" Roshayne yelled through the crack of the door. "There's a bomb in here! It's going to explode any second!"

We heard him yelling to someone else, "There's a bomb! Call the bomb squad and the fire department!"

A few seconds later, we heard another voice through the doorway.

"We're going to cut the padlock and force the door open! Stand back!" We heard the sound of bolt cutters snapping through the lock and several heavy crashes against the door. It didn't budge an inch. There was silence for a couple of seconds.

I looked closer at the door from the inside. "It looks like it's welded shut on this side!"

Somebody swore loudly. "We're coming through the wall!" he yelled. "Stand back!"

The whole building reverberated with the sounds of a heavy ax crashing against the corrugated metal. It was like being inside a huge steel drum, and we had to cover our ears against the onslaught. After several blows a hole started to form, and daylight spilled into the room. Gradually it grew bigger and bigger until the men outside had made almost a complete circle about three feet in diameter. Big, gloved hands grabbed the upper edges and, with extreme effort, began bending it outwards. Roshayne and I pushed as hard as we could from the inside.

"That's enough!" someone called out, and a uniformed policeman forced himself in through the jagged opening.

"Her first!" I shouted over the noise of the sprinkler and the alarm, pointing at Cindy. The officer and I dragged her to the hole and passed her through, head first, to the waiting arms. She was carried quickly away.

"Him next!" insisted Roshayne, rushing over to Paul. We passed him through the opening the same way. Roshayne went next and sprinted away from the building to the waiting emergency vehicles.

"Okay, son!" the policeman yelled in my ear. "Let's get out of here!"

I was just lowering my head to duck through when the bomb went off.

The sudden force from behind smashed my forehead against the crossbeam that ran just above the opening. My legs were blown out from under me, sending my whole body through the hole in a backwards somersault.

Ten feet out from the building, I left my body. I watched in horror as it crashed to the ground and cart-wheeled crazily along the pavement, coming to rest face up in a heap about forty feet from the hangar. Immediately behind me came a shower of hot, twisted metal and burning debris, flying through the air and pelting the ground for hundreds of feet in all directions. Paramedics and policemen dove to the ground, trying to protect themselves as best they could. Fortunately, Paul, Roshayne, and Cindy were behind an ambulance when the blast hit and were spared any further injury. For what seemed an eternity, the bits and pieces of the destroyed hangar rained down all around us.

I watched as several paramedics and policemen leaped to their feet and rushed into the mayhem. They grabbed my body by the wrists, and the bodies of three other men who had been close to the building, and dragged us quickly away from the burning building. I could see that some of my clothes were on fire. Another officer hurriedly rolled me over twice to extinguish the flames. Roshayne came running to my smoldering body.

I knew I needed to get back in, so I could get up. *Back to body!* I ordered myself.

Nothing happened.

Back to body! Back to body! I yelled again and again, but I couldn't get back in. The pull of the cord was no longer there. I tried lying on top of my body and sliding in, but I was pushed away like the opposing ends of two magnets.

What's going on? I cried out. *Why can't I get back in?*

Roshayne and several others were kneeling over my body. "Bart, come on! Get back in!" she yelled, looking around in the air. "You've got to get back in! Hurry, Bart!" She turned to one of the paramedics and told him forcefully, "He's just out of his body! He does it all the time! He'll come back! I know he will!"

A stretcher was brought over, and my body was lifted carefully onto it. In spite of the burns on my chest, the paramedics began doing CPR in an effort to revive me. Again I tried to get back in, but could not. I began to panic. *This can't be happening!* I screamed. *I can't be dead! Not now! Please, not now!*

As the paramedics continued their work, the stretcher was lifted and loaded into the waiting ambulance. Roshayne tried to get in also, but was pulled back by one of the paramedics. After the door was closed, the sirens and lights came on and it raced away, leaving me hovering by myself in midair.

CHAPTER 22

- The Angel -

As I watched the ambulance disappear, a feeling of despair and loneliness came over me. I felt that I had failed my friends. I just stood there helpless, wondering if I should follow and keep trying to get back in my body.

Then, through all the noise and confusion, I heard someone calling my name.

"Bartholomew. Bartholomew."

I wondered who could be calling, since my body had just been taken away. I looked around at all the paramedics and policemen, but they were busy fighting the fire and attending to the other injured men. Fire engines and more police cars were pulling into the area. Near the second ambulance, some men were attending to Paul, Roshayne, and Cindy.

"Bartholomew," it spoke again.

The voice was soft and powerful, and I realized that it wasn't coming from the ground at all. In fact, it wasn't even a verbal voice. It was the same kind of mental communication I had experienced with Jill in the hospital, and it penetrated my whole mind and soul.

I turned my attention from the ground to the sky and saw a most brilliant white light directly over my head. It was like nothing I had ever experienced, and, even though it was mid-day and the sun was out, the light made the sun look pale by comparison.

"Bartholomew, come to me," a voice said calmly from the center of the light.

It was exactly what I had expected to see and hear at the time of the accident, and I was convinced at that point that I was, in fact, dead. The cord had been severed. It was over.

I felt myself being drawn upwards. There was nothing I could have done to stop it. The light grew brighter and more intense as I was literally sucked into the middle of it. The noise and commotion below faded away, the sun disappeared, and I felt like I had been lifted right up into heaven.

As I came closer to the source of the voice, I was completely overcome with feelings of warmth, love, and compassion that totally defied description.

"Are you Christ?" I asked the voice.

I was surprised to realize that I was not the least bit nervous or afraid of him.

"I am an angel—a messenger on the Lord's errand," he answered.

Gradually, I could see the form of a man take shape, and it was obvious that he was not only the source of the voice, but the source of the light as well. He shone brilliantly, and the light radiated from him in all directions. When I was almost close enough to see his features, I stopped moving and he spoke to me again.

"Are you ready to move on, Bartholomew? Are you satisfied with your life?"

Before I could answer, an incredible thing happened. My entire life passed before my eyes, or through my mind—I wasn't sure which. I was still aware of the being standing in front of me, but at the same time I watched somehow, in living, three dimensional color, everything I had ever said, done, or even thought about. It flashed before me with such speed that it could only have been a matter of seconds by earth's time, and yet it was thorough and absolutely complete, down to the tiniest detail.

I saw myself as a little kid playing in the yard with my brother. I saw from my first day of kindergarten to my last day of junior high. I saw myself sitting on my Grandpa's knee before he died, and eating Grandma's homemade cookies. I saw all the good times I had spent with my family and friends.

I also saw the bad times. I saw myself teasing and tormenting my little sisters and fighting with my brothers. I saw myself yelling at my mother. I saw many things that I had done wrong, and I felt terrible about them. I wished I could go back and re-live those times and correct them.

Through it all, I never felt even the least bit intimidated or condemned by the personage in front of me. He just continued to pour out his love and compassion, acceptance and understanding.

At the end of the dramatic review, he asked me again, "Are you ready to move on, Bartholomew? Are you satisfied with your life?"

I wasn't sure what to say. I knew that whatever I said, it would be the truth. There was absolutely no way to lie to the angel. He knew my thoughts and my heart and soul inside and out. His question was intended more to cause me to examine myself and reflect on my life than to give him an answer that he already knew.

"I did the best I knew how at the time I did it," I answered, "but I know now that I could have done better if I had tried harder. I still have a lot to learn."

"Yes, you do," he answered simply. "Come with me."

I was aware, at that point, that we were separated by a thin, grayish-white curtain of mist, which seemed to be a dividing line of some sort. He motioned for me to move to my left, and as I did so he moved with me, but kept himself separated from me by the mist. I did not want to quit looking at him. It was such a wonderful feeling.

"Look there," he commanded, pointing to my left. I finally looked away and found myself standing in a big field, surrounded by beautiful trees and spectacular greenery. There was a beautiful crystal-blue lake in front of me. Beyond were rolling meadows filled with people dressed in white. They were in conversation with each other and casually moving about. It seemed to me that I should know some of those people, but I could not bring any names or faces into focus.

I also saw a gigantic white marble building, like a castle, nestled in the trees to the right of the meadow, and was left with the impression that it had been built just for me. The overall scene was majestic and splendid, and the feeling was one of absolute peace and tranquility. With every fiber of my being, I yearned to be able to cross over and become a part of it all. It truly felt as though I had returned home.

"This may be yours to enjoy now, if you choose. You will be free from the worries and pressures of the mortal world. You will find your rest and your reward."

I was surprised at his words. "I have a choice, then?"

"Look there," he said. I looked where he pointed and saw an ancient city with narrow cobblestone streets, surrounded by tall mountains. The streets were filled with people hurrying frantically in all directions, as though they were looking for something. They appeared to be dark-skinned, like South American or Polynesian, but were dressed in a very unusual way.

Before I could analyze the scene further, it changed and I was in another place with very wide roads and odd-shaped houses. The people were wearing robes, like in the bible pictures. Again and again I was transported mentally or spiritually from one place to another. I was taken rapidly in and out of dozens, maybe hundreds of houses. I saw people crying and raising their arms and carrying on, and I felt depressed and helpless. I witnessed a little crippled child and a blind man walking with a stick, and felt compassion for them. I stood by as a young boy thrashed around on a bed, banging against a wall like he was possessed with a devil, and felt angry with Satan and his hosts of devils. I saw a young girl lying unconscious in the midst of a raging fire, and wanted to reach in and pull her out. I saw many, many others—some so fast that I hardly had time to see them at all.

From there, I was escorted to a hilltop somewhere and saw the panoramic view of a vast, modern city all around me. I wondered if it was Salt Lake or Provo, but I couldn't see anything that looked familiar. I became aware of many other people around me, also looking out over the same valley and pointing at something. None of them seemed to be aware of my presence. I wondered who they were and why they were there with me. I was taken down into the valley and stopped in front of a red brick house with flowers and trees all around. I saw some small children playing in the yard and had the strangest feeling that they were my own—or at least could be someday.

As suddenly as it had begun, the trip was over, and I was aware again of the curtain of mist and the bright white angel on the other side.

"These are your choices, Bartholomew," he said softly. "If you choose, you may enter into your rest. Your mission in mortality would be over."

I thought about the peaceful meadow and felt again the almost uncontrollable urge to go there.

"Or," he continued, "you may return and finish walking the path that the Lord has chosen for you. Many are waiting for you and your gift, Bartholomew." He paused. "The choice is yours."

I thought about my father and mother and my brothers and sisters. I remembered my friends. I contemplated the future I had always dreamed about and hoped for—graduation, college, marriage, raising a family, a productive career.

Ol' Lady Owens' words came back to me again, sweet and crystal clear, as though I was hearing her feeble voice for the very first time.

"You have a gift, you know. A very special gift. I don't know exactly what it is, but the Spirit bore witness very strongly to me today that you are special. The Lord has given you something very precious and extremely rare. You will be a great blessing to many people, if you are humble and use it wisely. If you are selfish or use it thoughtlessly, the Lord will withdraw it from you. Be strong."

Having reflected on all those things, the decision was not hard to make. I didn't even have to communicate it to the angel before he spoke again.

"The Lord is pleased that your ambitions and motivations are unselfish. There will be many challenges ahead of you, Bartholomew. You must strengthen your faith in order to be equal to the task. You must be firm and unflinching.

"You must also understand, Bartholomew, that your mortal body has suffered greatly. It will be painful for you going back, but in due time your body will heal. Is it your desire to return?"

"Yes," I said without hesitation.

I decided then and there that if God had a work for me to do, I was going to do it—no matter what. I knew he would help me.

"Yes, that is what I want," I confirmed.

No sooner did I say the words than the angel began to draw away from me. As he moved backwards, the light seemed to draw in around him, like a curtain being pulled. I noticed the darkness of space coming in around me, and stars began to appear. I looked again at the angel and watched as he grew smaller and smaller until he appeared as just another bright star in the sky.

I was amazed to see that all the stars seemed to be following him. They were coming from behind me and passing over my head and under my feet. They moved faster and faster, until they were practically just a blur of light.

Then I realized that it was not the angel or the stars that were moving. It was me. I was traveling backwards through space at something close to the speed of light. I had no idea where I was going, but I did not want to turn around. I wanted to see the angel and the light, and feel the warmth of his love on my face for as long as possible.

Gradually, the stars slowed their pace and it became light again. Not the brilliant white light of the angel, but the soft, pale blue of the earth's sky. The stars faded out and gave way to the light of the sun. My rate of travel slowed down as I drew nearer to the earth, and I saw billowy white clouds come and go. Seeing the clouds, my sense of direction changed from going backwards to going down. Still I did not want to turn around. I felt as though I was being lowered gently to the ground in the strong hands of a loving father, and I had absolutely no fear or sensation of falling at all.

There was a brief blackout as I was lowered through a roof, then I came to a stop, staring up into some bright white lights. I could sense that my body was immediately beneath me. It seemed God was cradling me there in his hands, like a newborn baby, taking one last look at me before letting me go back to mortality.

I looked around and saw that I was in a hospital emergency room. Off to one side stood a nurse, somberly arranging some things on a tray. Behind her stood the two paramedics who had loaded my body into the ambulance. They looked desperately tired and dejected. There were other nurses and attendants moving all around me.

Over my shoulder, I saw one wrapping up and storing away electrical paddles used for shocking the heart. Over the other shoulder, I recognized the green monitor and saw the steady flat line streaming across the screen. Someone else lifted an air bag and extracted a tube from my throat below me, then hung it on a hook.

"It's over," I heard the doctor announce. "He's gone. It's been over thirty minutes since the paramedics initiated CPR. No one is revived after that long a time. Even if he was, he would be a vegetable for the rest of his life." He looked at the paramedics and other personnel in the room and added softly, "I'm sorry."

I felt myself being lowered the last few inches into my body. I strained and strained, and finally managed to open my physical eyes a little bit—just in time to see the white sheet being pulled up over my head.

"Mark the time," the doctor said. "He's dead."

CHAPTER 23

- The Abyss -

My fifteen thousand and one body parts were slow to realize that there was again a living, functioning spirit inhabiting the space, and a mind and brain that needed their reports. After the brief delayed reaction, they simultaneously transmitted their thousands and millions of responses from every nerve end, tissue, bone, muscle, and internal organ. The heart began again to pump life's blood through the veins, and the muscles responded to commands and instincts.

I felt suddenly as if I was lying in a lake of molten lava. I was startled by the blood-curdling scream that came involuntarily from my own lips, and grew louder and louder. My arms and legs jerked violently out from the sides of the table, sending the sheet flying and knocking the I.V. stand to the floor. My neck and spine arched upwards, lifting my shoulders and back from the table. Every muscle and tendon in my body went as tight as a violin string. The screaming was ear splitting and relentless.

There was so much pain! I never knew there could BE so much pain! Spasm after spasm coursed relentlessly through my entire body, and it became a quivering, jerking mass of injured, broken, burned, cut, and bleeding parts and pieces.

At the first sound of the screams, everyone jumped, then stood frozen in place, stunned beyond belief at the sudden outburst and the hideous sight of my body thrashing wildly on the table, shaking and pulsing and arching.

The screams went on and on.

The paramedics were shocked. Never in their careers had they seen anything so hideous.

The nurse standing by the door slammed into her tray and sent paraphernalia careening off walls and floors and cabinets, adding to the cacophony of noise. She backed up hard against the wall and fell to the floor in the sitting position. Then she crab-walked along the floor, turned over on all fours, scrambled to her feet, and raced out the door, where she collided head-on with another nurse. They both screamed.

After the initial shock, everyone jumped as one, grabbing my arms and legs, ignoring the burns and broken bones in a desperate attempt to restrain me and keep me from falling off the table.

Still the screams continue unabated and reverberated through the corridors. Orders were shouted by everyone to everyone. Nurses, normally accustomed to the stress of the emergency room, were running and shouting, and collided with each other. More people came rushing into the room.

Finally, lost and unnoticeable among the overwhelming, all-encompassing pain, a needle was jabbed to the hilt into my arm and its contents dispensed. The screams and convulsions continued for several more seconds before the medication finally took hold.

Then, as quickly and as suddenly as it had all started, the screaming stopped. The silence that followed was total, broken only by the steady beat of the heart monitor. Nobody dared breathe. Everyone stood perfectly still, waiting expectantly for the hideous noise to start again.

After feeling as though my entire body had been burning up in a blast furnace, the sudden rush of cold that coursed through my body from the injection was like being thrown into the icy arctic deep. My muscles relaxed again and my back settled slowly to the table. My lips quivered and my eyelids fluttered. My fingers twitched and curled up into a loose fist. My arms and legs hung limp.

Then I felt what seemed to be the soothing, rocking motion of the ocean, sweeping me gently from side to side as I slowly settled to the bottom. The deeper I went, the darker it got, until gradually the blackness enveloped me completely, and the world around me ceased to exist. Then, it was total nothingness. Deep, dark, empty nothingness.

How long I was unconscious or asleep was impossible to determine. As I gradually came back to my senses, I became vaguely aware of faraway voices, muffled and indistinct. I felt myself being moved back and forth, and being turned over and over. I lost track of whether I was face up or face down. The darkness continued, but with varying shades of blue and gray. After a long time, the dim light was interrupted by a bright kaleidoscope of colors that flashed brilliantly for several seconds, then disappeared.

After another undetermined amount of time, the pain returned. It started as a throbbing in my fingertips and spread to my hands and arms, and on down through my entire body. Soon it felt as though the veins in my neck would explode. My body ignited again with the same searing heat as before, and I attempted to move my limbs to get up and escape. When the pain became unbearable, the screams started—and soon I felt the pinprick of a needle somewhere in my body. The throbbing subsided, and I was hurtled again into the cold and soothing deep. The relief felt wonderful, and I wanted nothing more than to stay at the bottom of the dark abyss forever.

The cycle repeated itself over and over again, with only minor variations. Darkness, movements and voices, rising to the dim lights, bright colors, the heat of the furnace, intense pain, screams . . . then needles, the cold ocean, sinking back to the bottom, and darkness. I lost all sense of time. Minutes became hours. Hours became days. Days became weeks. It felt as though I had been tossed about in the rising and dropping tide of pain for an infinity, like a piece of forgotten driftwood, beating against the reefs and cliffs, then being swept back out to sea, again and again.

Then, on one ascent, I became aware of a steadily growing pinpoint of blue light, like the sun shining on the surface hundreds of feet above me. I wanted desperately to reach the light and see the sky and the sun again. I struggled and groaned and tried to swim, amazed that I hadn't drowned already. The more I swam, the less it felt like water, and I wondered if I was actually floating into the sky. I couldn't tell if I was in my body or out. The light grew larger and flickered and danced. The colors changed slowly from deep blue to light turquoise, and then to yellowish white. I heard sounds, like waves breaking on a beach.

I felt suddenly as buoyant as a submerged beach ball and shot through the surface and out into the brilliant open sky like a torpedo. The light was blinding. The rocking motion of the deep disappeared, and I sensed that I was lying on solid ground again. Strangely, I was neither hot nor cold. The fire had finally been extinguished.

As I tried to focus on something, I became aware that my eyes were closed and wondered how I had been seeing the lights and colors all that time. I tried to force them open, but they were stuck fast. I concentrated on forcing one eyelid up, and felt it move a fraction of an inch. The light that came through was excruciating, and I closed it quickly. I repeated the exercise with the other eyelid with the same results.

Over and over I forced them open, a little more each time, until they gradually adjusted to the light. Finally I had them both open wide, and was ready to see where I was.

I stared up into the sky and noticed that it was a dark gray color. I concluded that it must be early morning or late evening. I could see tiny pinpoints of black, which surprised me. I didn't understand why the stars weren't white. There were dark black parallel lines running overhead, like looking up through power lines.

I wanted to locate the source of the light I had seen. I tried to turn my head to the side, but my body and brain were slow in figuring out how to work together again. I had to blink many, many times before I could clear the water from my eyes and hold things in focus.

It's a fluorescent light fixture, I thought, surprised. *How could that be?*

I turned back and stared into the sky again. Gradually, I came to realize that it wasn't a sky at all. It was a ceiling, covered with acoustic tile.

Where am I? How did I get here? What am I doing here? I tried desperately to remember.

What happened before the ocean and the furnace? How long have I been here in this room?

There did not appear to be any answers. Just more and more questions. I concentrated harder, and vaguely remembered hearing someone screaming.

Was that me? I wondered.

Like a slow motion video, the images finally began to appear. I recalled seeing people dressed in white walking around, and a big white building. Then the people in white turned into doctors and nurses, and I remembered being lowered into an emergency room. The doctor had pronounced me dead.

I cast my eyes around as far as possible without moving my head again. *This doesn't look like the emergency room. It's a private hospital room.*

The images of a valley and a large city came to mind. Then an airport and a large airplane. The images were swirling around and getting all mixed together, and I was having great difficulty sorting them out.

I was trying to figure out the meaning of an explosion and a man holding a gun when I heard a noise. It was a sigh, followed by steady, heavy breathing.

Someone else is in the room! I realized.

I wasn't sure if I should be afraid or not. It came from the side opposite the light fixture. I twisted my neck and head around to see. There appeared to be a figure back in the shadows, slumped down in an armchair. He looked as if he was sleeping.

Or is it a woman? I blinked several times again and strained to focus.

It's my mom!

My heart filled with warmth, and tears blurred my vision again. I opened my mouth and tried to call her, but no sound came out. My mouth felt like it was full of cotton balls. I moved my tongue around and tried to swallow, to work up some moisture. I tried again and heard a faint squeaky croaking noise. The heavy breathing stopped, and I saw her head come up, looking in my direction. One last time, I tried to form the word.

"Mom?"

It came out in an almost inaudible whisper, but she heard it loud and clear. Instantly, she sprang to her feet and rushed to my side.

"Bart?" she said, choking on her words. "Oh, my dear, sweet baby! You're awake!" Tears began to fall. "Oh, thank the Lord! You're finally awake!"

CHAPTER 24

- Answers -

It was a little after four in the morning when I came to, and for the next few hours I felt like I was a sideshow in a circus. Dad showed up about an hour later, and from then until about nine or ten, doctors and nurses came in and out by the dozens.

They asked me all kinds of questions, and poked and prodded me in every place imaginable. They took my temperature, my pulse, and my blood pressure. They checked my eyes and ears and throat. They made me bend all my fingers and toes, and checked my reflexes.

And then they embarrassed me to death when they yanked the sheet right off the bed to replace all the bandages and give me a sponge bath. I protested loudly.

"It's way too late to be embarrassed, Bart," a pretty young nurse informed me. "We've been doing this for days already."

"What do you mean 'days already'?" I asked, trying desperately to concentrate on something besides the cold, wet sponge. "How long have I been here?"

The nurse glanced at the doctor in the corner, realizing she had said something out of turn.

He smiled and came over to the side of the bed. "You've been here with us for . . . let's see," he calculated in his head, "twenty-five days now."

"Twenty-five days?" I repeated. "I've been out for TWENTY-FIVE DAYS?" I couldn't believe my ears. "What day is it?"

"Thanksgiving is tomorrow," Mom informed me. "We got our first real snow yesterday. About eight inches. We've been praying earnestly that you would be up in time for our big turkey dinner."

"I'm afraid that won't be possible," replied the doctor. "He's going to have to stay here for another couple of weeks. There are some minor surgical procedures that still need to be done, and the risk of infection is still too great."

As the day progressed, I learned that I had suffered a major concussion from the blow to the head, and there had been some worry about whether I might lose my eyesight. My eyes had been covered for several days.

That explained the darkness. The doctor told me later that the bright colored lights I had seen were a normal part of the healing process. I had also suffered some sprains and broken bones from the tumble on the asphalt, but most of them were pretty well healed up already.

The head trauma and the burns to my chest and legs had caused the majority of the pain. What had kept me under for so many days had been the pain medications. I soon found out that there was plenty more pain to come, but at least I was able to endure it without being rendered unconscious by drugs again. I mostly just slept for the next couple of days anyway.

On Thanksgiving Day at around mid-day, Mom and Dad brought Darin and Charlene and Cynthia with their hands full of Thanksgiving dinner. The big surprise was a huge piece of Mom's famous pumpkin pie, hand delivered by none other than my big brother Chris.

"Good to see you, worm," he said. "I was afraid I would have to start picking on Darin, if you didn't hurry back."

Mom told me Chris had decided, out of the blue, to come and find us for the holidays. I think he finally got homesick, but he would never admit it. He brought a weird, shabbily dressed girl with him, and they came the whole way from California on his motorbike. Mom about had a heart attack.

The word got out. Starting Friday, the whole place turned into Grand Central Station. Since it was a holiday weekend, everybody under the sun decided to come and see me. Paul and Roshayne were first.

"Boy, it's good to see you awake again," Paul said, trying to control his emotions. "We were beginning to wonder if you were EVER coming back."

"I've been praying for you twenty times a day," Roshayne threw in, her eyes moist. "You don't know how lucky you are, Bart. Actually it's a miracle WE'RE alive, when you think about it."

"I'm not sure I understand," I said confused. "What . . . what happened?"

They both looked at me with blank expressions.

"You mean you don't remember?" Roshayne asked in surprise. "You don't remember the bomb?"

Before I could answer, the next wave of visitors flooded into the crowded room.

"Hey, it's the hero of the year!" said Neil. "Good to see you again, buddy."

"Hero?" I asked.

"Yeah," he answered. "For catching all the bad guys."

"You're looking good," Scott added. "You know, considering."

"Considering what?" I asked.

"All the bandages," he answered, "and that punk hospital haircut."

"I think it's kind of cute," Roshayne said with a chuckle.

Gradually, in a disjointed sort of way, the events of that fateful Saturday were reviewed, and all the details discussed until I finally had a good idea of what had occurred. It took several days before some of their information was confirmed by my own memory. For the time being, I had to pretty much take their word for it. I noticed that there was nothing said about any out-of-body stuff. I quietly asked Roshayne about that, first chance I got.

"People don't know ALL the facts, Bart," she whispered. "Don't worry. The gift is secure."

By the end of the day, I had enough flowers and cards in the room to open my own floral shop.

Monday, I got another surprise. Neil poked his head in the door and whistled softly to get my attention. "Hey, Bart," he said with a grin on his face, "you up for a special visitor?"

"Sure," I answered, trying to see around the corner. He went back out and pushed a wheelchair through the door.

"Jill! You . . . you're awake!"

"I was about to say the same about you," she said, smiling. "You look great, Bart."

"I was about to say the same about you!" I replied.

We all laughed.

"Bart," she said, looking around the room to make sure we were alone, "I want to thank you for coming to visit me."

"You remember that?" I asked, surprised.

"Well, at first I thought it had been a dream or something, but when I told Neil about it, he told me what you had done . . . and about your . . . ability."

I didn't know what to say.

"I took your advice," Neil said. "Well, actually it was Jill's advice, wasn't it? I've been working things out. So has Jill. Things are going to be better."

"I'm glad."

"Thanks, Bart," Jill said. "We owe you."

"It was nothing."

"It was a lot more than nothing. Come and see me when they give you your wheels," she said, pointing at her wheelchair. "I'm up one floor."

Later that same afternoon, a man and a lady and a girl I had never seen before came into the room. Mom and Dad came in behind them.

"Bart Elderberry?" he asked.

"Yeah, that's me."

"My name is Doug Fenton. This is my wife, Liz, and my daughter, Andrea."

"Andrea?" I asked stupidly. "Andrea! You're Andrea! The one in the pictures—I mean newspapers." She giggled shyly.

"YOU'RE the one in the papers these days," responded Mrs. Fenton. "You've been on national TV, in every paper in the state, and even hit CNN Headline News."

"I did?"

"I can't tell you how happy I am that you caught those evil men who kidnapped my daughter," Mr. Fenton said.

"I did?"

He put his arm around Andrea's shoulders. "As a token of our appreciation, I am personally delivering your reward." I glanced nervously at Andrea and caught her eye briefly before she blushed and looked at the floor.

You've got to be kidding.

Mr. Fenton saw the exchange and laughed. "No. Not her, Bart," he exclaimed. "This." He pulled an envelope from his pocket and handed it to me.

I opened it and gasped. "It's a check! For fifty thousand dollars!" I could barely get the words out.

"Well, actually, it's not a check," he explained. "Your parents wouldn't let me give you a cash reward, so I compromised." I waited expectantly. "It's a trust fund that's been set up in your name."

"It'll be for college, of course," Mom said, reading the greedy look in my eyes.

"And whatever's left, you get when you're twenty-five or married, whichever comes first," Dad added.

"I don't know what to say," I replied.

"It's the least we could do," Mrs. Fenton said.

I turned to Andrea. "Did they keep you in the same room that Cindy was in?"

"Yes," she answered. "I've talked with Cindy a few times. They treated me a lot better than they did her."

"I'm glad."

I couldn't think of anything else to say, and there was an uncomfortable silence.

"Well, we'd better get going," Mr. Fenton said, saving us. "You're a very brave boy, Bart."

"Or a very foolish one," Mom corrected him.

It was six days after I woke up before I finally got a chance to talk with Roshayne and Paul in private, and find out exactly what had happened after the blast. They made it a point to come when no one else would be there, and brought Tamara and Cindy with them.

Paul told the story. "After they took us all to the hospital, the police came and asked us all kinds of questions. We told them right away about the plane and Mr. Clawson's plans to go to Mexico. They enlisted some help from the Nellis Air Force Base in Nevada. A couple of jet pilots spotted them before they were able to cross the border and forced them down to the nearest airport. The FBI found close to four million dollars in cash on board."

"Four million?" I asked. "Where did they get the extra million?"

"From the six guys they were blackmailing. They gave Mr. Fenton his entire three million back. The rest is still in limbo until they sort everything out. Evidently, most of those guys were not exactly squeaky clean. There was bank fraud and some other high level stuff going on that Mr. Clawson found out about. Most of them have also been arrested and are under investigation."

"How did the police find out about all the blackmail stuff?" I asked. "Did they find the books?"

"I gave them the one you found in Tiffany's locker," answered Roshayne, "and the others turned up all by themselves, complete with all the photos, disks, and printouts."

"Where?"

"Tiffany had stashed them in her gym locker in her backpack. Apparently it never occurred to Derek or Silver Hawk to look there. Miss Thompson, the P.E. teacher, found them when she cleaned out Tiffany's stuff, and turned them over to the police."

"Where are they now?" I asked. "Clawson and Hawk, I mean."

Paul answered, "Mr. Clawson, Silver Hawk, Derek, and the pilot were all arrested on the spot, and are being held in the Utah County jail, without bail, for murder, attempted murder, kidnapping, arson, blackmail and a dozen other things." I lay back and let all this news soak in for a couple of minutes in silence.

"I've been wondering," I said finally. "When I left my body, there were some other guys on the ground by the hangar. Cops or paramedics. What happened to them?"

"There were three guys standing outside the building when the bomb went off," Paul answered. "They were all knocked flat by the blast and suffered some minor burns and broken bones. Since their clothes weren't soaked with gas like ours, they were easier to take care of."

There was an awkward pause. Cindy spoke up for the first time. "The policeman who came in to help us get out is . . . dead, Bart," she said softly. "His name was Adam Carmichael. He was twenty-nine years old. Married with two little girls. They gave him a big military-like funeral. In my opinion, he's the hero. The Governor gave his family a medal."

That news left me stunned. No one spoke for several moments.

Roshayne asked, "Bart? What did you mean when you said 'I left my body'? Did you jump out after the bomb? Why did you take so long to come back?"

"You were pronounced dead in the emergency room," Paul interjected. "You went without a heartbeat for—"

"—more than thirty minutes," I finished. "I know. I was watching. I had a Near Death Experience."

"Very funny," Paul said.

"I'm serious, Paul. I had an honest-to-goodness NDE, complete with the light, the angel, and the whole works."

I spent the next several minutes reliving my sacred experience with them. They were all noticeably touched as I spoke, and no one made any attempt to hide their tears. At least they were tears of joy, for once.

"Bart, that's the most wonderful thing I've ever heard," Roshayne said reverently when I had finished.

"There's more," I said. I proceeded to tell them about my infinity spent in the dark and cold abyss, and all the pain I had suffered, right up to waking up on Wednesday morning.

"You are an amazing person," Cindy said for all of them. "Simply amazing."

"There's one thing I haven't figured out," Roshayne said. "How did the police get there so fast? They were already showing up at the airport before we even set off the sprinkler system. And where was the fire department?"

I looked at Tamara. "You haven't told them?"

"I thought they knew," she answered innocently.

"Knew what?" Paul and Roshayne asked together.

I smiled. "First, tell me what happened after Hawk ran out of the room in the 'jail' house," I asked. "After you got caught."

Paul scratched his chin. "Let's see. He ran out when he sensed you in the room, then he came right back in and told Mr. Clawson something like 'the little blankety-blanks have an invisible friend, but he left before I could see him.' They decided to set a trap for you."

"I tried to warn you when you came back and appeared to us," Roshayne reminded me. "Then all of a sudden it looked like you were hit hard from behind. You flew right through us with a shocked look on your face."

I related to them how Silver Hawk and I had fought out-of-body and about my subsequent race down the freeway.

"After Derek had taped me to the chair, and we were on our way to the airport, it occurred to me . . . 'Hawk is driving Derek's car, so he can't jump out right now.' I got out myself right away. Derek had actually done me a favor by strapping me in so well. There was absolutely no way I was going to fall out of that chair."

"What did you do out-of-body?" Roshayne asked breathlessly. "After you got out."

"I went and showed myself to the only other person I could think of who already knew about my ability," I answered.

"Me," announced Tamara excitedly, bouncing up and down. "He nearly scared me to death, I might add."

"She was pretty shook up," I remembered.

"Well, what do you expect?" she defended herself. "I'd never seen you do that before. And you caught me in the fitting room. I was with my mom at the mall in Orem," she explained. "I was just about to try on a dress at Mervyns when 'Casper the Friendly Ghost' here pops up in the mirror and starts yelling at me!" They all laughed.

"I had to wait until you were alone," I told her. "I couldn't very well show up in the middle of the ladies' clothes section with a dozen people around, could I? She screamed bloody murder," I added, turning to the others.

"My mom thought I had slipped and killed myself, and came practically climbing over the door."

"I had to disappear for a few minutes until she could calm her down," I said. "Then I told her everything that was going on, as fast as I could, and sent her running to a phone. I told her to tell them we were being held hostage by Tiffany's killers, and that they were going to try to get away from the Provo airport."

"Calling was the hardest part," Tamara continued, "because I had to lose my mom first so she wouldn't stand over my shoulder and listen. I told her I felt a sudden bout of diarrhea coming on and raced all the way through the mall to the restroom first," she laughed at herself, and we all joined in. Suddenly serious, she added, "If I had gotten to a phone quicker, that policeman might still be alive."

"You can't blame yourself for that," I told her. "You did the best you could have possibly done, and you saved all our lives in the process. If the police hadn't come when they did, we would be as flat as that hangar." A thought suddenly occurred to me. "Paul, what about your brother's van?"

"It's a Krispy-Kritter now," he answered, laughing, "but I don't feel too bad, knowing Mr. Clawson's Cadillac and Derek's convertible went with it."

CHAPTER 25

- Big Pigs -

About a week after Thanksgiving, I was finally allowed to go home. The doctor told me I would have to convalesce until the Christmas holidays.

That Sunday evening around the dinner table, I told my family about my visit with the angel and my Near Death Experience. Dad just sat there dumbfounded, amazed that he had actually fathered someone worthy of such an experience. Mom cried the whole way through. Charlene and Cynthia soaked it all in like little sponges, then plastered me with their usual hundred questions. Darin looked on in awe and admiration, as if I was a movie star or something. He treated me a bit differently after that.

It was a tender and special experience for the entire family. I wished Chris could have been there, but he and his girlfriend had returned to California.

On the following Monday, I was introduced to the GJBBN club—the "Get Jill & Bart Back to Normal" club—which consisted of Neil, Roshayne, Paul, Scott, Tamara, and Cindy. For the next month, right up until the end of the semester, they all took turns visiting Jill and me, tutoring us rigorously every night after school.

After a few days, I didn't see much of Neil anymore. He concentrated his efforts on Jill. Oddly enough, after about the same number of days, Jill didn't see much of Roshayne, either. The other four traded back and forth pretty regularly.

Paul got more and more attached to Tamara along the way, which didn't surprise me. And lucky Scott won the heart of Cindy, the most popular junior varsity cheerleader of the quarter. By the end of the month, we had pretty much filled Scott in on all the details. He felt really left out and jealous at having missed out on everything—except the accident, of course.

The holidays were cool—or should I say cold? Chris came back again, but in his girlfriend's car instead of on the motorcycle. They about froze to death riding back to California after Thanksgiving, and by Christmas there was another foot of snow on the ground. It was the first time in my life I had been able to experience a white Christmas.

The second semester went by pretty uneventfully, especially when compared to the first one. I was a celebrity again for the first few days after I got back to school, but everybody forgot about me pretty quick with basketball games and dances and such occupying their minds.

I made it a point not to use the gift for a while. I have to admit, I was more than a little worried about Silver Hawk. I knew that even though I had won the battle, the war was far from over. No prison walls were going to keep his spirit locked up. Occasionally I felt his presence, but he seemed to come less and less frequently over time. I hoped he would just forget about me and my dull high school life, but there was always that fear deep down inside.

Oh, there was one little incident. How could I forget. About a week after Valentines Day, I had my second run in with the Big Pigs. Roshayne and Paul and I had stayed late after school working on a project. We assumed by that time that we were the only ones in the hallway. We were talking and laughing, and as I stepped away from my locker, I collided with the Big Pigs head-on.

Talk about déjà vu city! There they were. Same hats. Same boots. Same humongous belt buckles.

"HEY! What's the big idea?" the leader complained. "Why don't you guys watch—" He stopped as recognition settled in. "Well, if it isn't the skinny little runt!" he said, sticking his thumbs in their usual places. "I warned you 'bout gettin' in our way again, didn't I, runt?"

I was too busy trying to keep my cool to think of anything cool to say.

He shoved me hard in the chest with both hands, knocking me back a foot or so.

"DIDN'T I, RUNT?!" he roared. He shoved me again a little harder, and I tried to knock his hands away. That was all he needed.

"YOU'RE DEAD!!" he yelled.

He grabbed me by the lapels of my jacket, lifted me off my feet, and literally threw me against the lockers.

My head banged hard against the locker door, and I slid slowly to the floor, seeing stars. Paul rushed in to help, but two of the cowboys grabbed him by the arms and held him back.

"Why don't you guys mind your own business?!" Roshayne yelled at the leader. "He hasn't done anything to you!"

The third guy grabbed her by the arms from behind and held her still.

The leader turned to look at her. "Well, ain't you a peach," he said. "You think you're gonna save the runt, do ya?" He glanced back at me. "Too late. He's out of it." He sauntered over to her with his hands on his hips, acting feminine. "So, now what? You gonna punch us out or somethin', sweetie cakes?" He laughed.

"Leave her alone!" Paul yelled.

"Leave her alone!" I echoed, jumping to my feet.

"Shut up!" the leader yelled at Paul, giving him a hard punch in the stomach.

Paul crumpled forward gasping for breath, but was held in place by his two captors. The Big Pig grabbed Roshayne hard by the jaw and twisted her head up sideways. He leaned over real close and said, "How abouts you 'n me goes someplace and haves ourselves some fun!" His left hand started caressing down her side and hips as she squirmed and struggled.

"You jerk!!" I yelled. I ran over to pull him away. When I grabbed his shoulders, my hands went right through and closed on themselves. *"What—?"*

"I'd rather die!" Roshayne breathed into his face.

The other pigs started laughing. The leader's eyes got red and mad, and he grabbed her away from the third guy and pulled her into a tight bear hug, trying to kiss her. Roshayne twisted her head from side to side and kicked him in the shins.

"Let her go!!" I yelled, as loud as I could. Nobody paid any attention. Suddenly it occurred to me that no one was seeing or hearing me. *I must have bounced out when I hit the locker,* I realized.

Light and visible! I commanded myself, not wanting to waste time getting back in my body. "Get your filthy hands off!!" I yelled at the top of my lungs.

He spun his head around and looked me square in the eye.

"I'm the one you want," I said. "Come and get me!"

In a flash, he let Roshayne go and charged full tilt. Of course, instead of knocking me off my feet, as was his intention, he ran straight through thin air, promptly lost his balance, and stumbled to the floor. The two guys holding Paul, thinking I had dodged their leader somehow, dropped Paul and charged. The third guy came at me hard from the opposite direction.

What was intended to be a full-scale, no-holds-barred, football tackle resulted in a violent head-on collision, and they bounced off of each other like bowling pins. They all fell helter-skelter to the floor and looked around dazed, rubbing their heads. The leader sat up and stared at me wide eyed, then glanced nervously back and forth between me and my inert body on the floor right beside him.

I was mad.

"Where do you guys come off thinking you can push people around like that?" I yelled at them. "You think you own the place?" I moved down close and hovered in the air right over the Big Pig. "You think you're so tough?!—you and you're stupid friends?!"

He crawled backwards and sprawled out flat on the floor, his eyes wide with fear.

"You think you can go around playing with girls like they're your own private toy or something?!" I demanded heatedly. "You think you can just clobber any ol' guy that looks at you cross-eyed? You think you're the almighty King of the Jungle or something? Well, you're wrong!!" I yelled, coming down to within inches of his face. "You have no right!! Absolutely no right!!"

He scrambled backwards in an attempt to get away from me. The other guys, seeing their leader down and defenseless and my body lying still on the floor, realized that I was not what I appeared to be and backed away in fear.

Seeing that I had the advantage, I continued. "Everybody's sick and tired of you jerks terrorizing this school! You're all a bunch of wimps! Spineless cowards hiding behind your big hats and boots and your tuff-guy act!"

I rose slowly up into the air, until my head was at ceiling level and looked at the four of them one at a time with my arms crossed and eyebrows furrowed. I let them sweat for a few seconds as my eyes burned deep. They all held their breath.

"Get out of here!!" I yelled suddenly, making them all jump, "before I REALLY get mad!!" I pointed down the hall at the doors.

The leader sprang to his feet and raced down the hall. The other three were on the wrong side of me and had to inch their way along the lockers until they were sure they were clear. Then they bolted as one and crashed through the door behind their leader and out into the raging blizzard.

For several seconds we remained still, trying to calm down and allowing our adrenaline to slow back down to normal.

"Are you guys okay?" I asked finally.

Roshayne leaned over and helped Paul to his feet. "Where's Bart?" she asked, looking up and down the hall. Their eyes finally rested on my body.

I'm invisible again, I realized. *Back to body!*

Slowly I let my eyes flicker open, then sat up, rubbing my head. "What . . . what happened?" I asked, innocently.

"Very funny," Roshayne said.

"Boy, that was out of control!" Paul said in awe.

"Yeah, I guess maybe I got a little carried away," I answered. "I just freaked out when I saw—"

"No, it was fantastic!" Paul exclaimed. "It was . . . you were—"

"Out-of-body," I finished for him.

"Jeeze, Bart," he said reverently. "That was the most awesome thing I've ever seen in my whole life."

"Thanks, Bart," Roshayne said sincerely. They both reached down and hauled me to my feet. "Getting out of your body was really smart, you know. How did you do it so fast?"

"I didn't really do it on purpose," I explained. "I guess I left my body when I hit the locker." I brushed off my pants and we stood there looking at each other. "Kind of gives whole new meaning to the term 'being knocked out', though, doesn't it?"

We all burst out laughing as we walked arm in arm down the hall. The Big Pig had left his hat behind on the floor, which I proudly claimed as my trophy.

Every time the Big Pigs saw us after that, they made an abrupt about-face and took off the way they'd come.

Well, the year finally came to an end, and all of a sudden it was yearbook day. I asked the guys to meet me in the gymnasium during lunch. When I had them all together, I popped the big announcement on them.

"I'm moving again, you guys."

"What? Where?" they asked in surprise.

"My dad decided he didn't like the country so much after all. We're going to be moving to Orem in about three weeks. As soon as we sign the papers on our new house."

"Oh, Bart!" Roshayne exclaimed. "Why?"

I thought she was going to cry right there in front of everybody. She grabbed my yearbook out of my hands, sat down, and proceeded to write her life's story in it. I was afraid I would never get it back.

Paul finally got to add his two bits' worth during our last bus ride home.

"Well, Bart," he said, just before we got to his stop, "it's been an interesting experience, knowing you."

"That's probably the understatement of the year," I confessed.

"Don't be a stranger," he said as he got off the bus. "See you Sunday in church."

Later, in my room, I settled down to read what Roshayne had written in my yearbook. I was about half done reading her entry when I heard the doorbell ring.

"Bart!" Mom called. "There's someone here for you."

It was Roshayne.

"Hi, Bart," she said, nervously. "I know I'll probably see you around a few more times, but . . ." she paused and took a deep breath. "I just wanted to come by and tell you in person . . ." She stopped again and looked around me into the house to make sure there were no witnesses present.

"I love you, Bart," she said quickly.

Without warning, she threw her arms around me, pulled my head down with one hand, and planted the biggest kiss I had ever had—right on the lips!

Okay, so actually it was the ONLY kiss I had ever had, but who's counting?

My yearbook slipped from my hands and tumbled to the floor. After an eternity of sheer bliss—at least four whole seconds—she broke off, turned, and ran to her car. She was gone before I knew what had happened.

After I had properly recovered, I finished reading her entry.

" . . . and Bart, don't forget about your gift. God gave it to you for a purpose: To bless people's lives. I know you haven't done much with it lately, but I'm confident that you will in the future. You have the ability to make people laugh and enjoy life. You know how to give people a reason to keep trying. You can protect people from evil. You can remind people of their purpose in life. You can strengthen people's character. You can even save people's lives. You inspire people to love and care.

"I know . . . because you did all those things for me, and more. I'll love you always. —Rosh."

EPILOGUE

It's been over a year now since that exciting and tragic year. I still see the gang every once in a while at football games and such, and we enjoy reminiscing over old times. In the meantime, I've been active in all sorts of extracurricular activities and preparing hard for my last year in high school. All in all, life has been good.

One of my favorite pastimes now is to camp out by myself up Payson Canyon. I've made it a point to go at least every three months. I like to go by myself, when the weather is cooperative, so I can camp without a tent. I like to lie out in the open air and stare into the sky until the wee hours of the morning. I pray to God for strength to carry on. I ask for forgiveness for all the stupid things I've done. I reflect on my goals in life and try to sort out whatever problems I've been dealing with.

Then I concentrate on the stars. I love the stars. I try to imagine which of those thousands and millions of blinking, glistening specks of light is my guardian angel.

"I'm trying to be strong," I tell him out loud. "I'm trying to be firm. I'm trying to do the best I can, and I know that I can still do better if I try harder. I still have a lot to learn."

"Yes, you do, Bartholomew," I imagine him answering back. "Indeed, you do."

About the Author

Brent "BJ" Rowley is a man of varied interests who describes himself as an enterprising entrepreneur—someone determined to experience life to its fullest. He has a diverse background in such things as real estate developement and construction, commercial explosives, venture capital brokerage, and music composing and recording, to mention only a few. BJ currently works fulltime as a network engineer.

Writing young-adult fiction is a relatively new interest recently added to his list.

"I enjoy adventure stories about exciting and interesting things that could possibly happen to normal, everyday people," he says.

My Body Fell Off! (also formerly published as *Light Traveler: The Adventure Begins*) is his first novel.

BJ also enjoys photography, aviation, playing the piano, and spending time with his family. He lives with his wife and the youngest three of his five children in Orem, Utah.

BJ would love to hear from his readers. You can write to him via e-mail at:

fanmail@bjrowley.com

Or visit his website: http://www.bjrowley.com

He may also be contacted by writing in care of Golden Wings Enterprises: P.O. Box 468, Orem, Utah 84059-0468

Author's Note

Since the original publication of this adventure series (under two different titles), I have received varying degrees of criticism from a few individuals and organizations about the implications of depicting Astral Projection as a "Gift from God." And many have wondered about my incentive and motivation to write these stories the way I did. I would therefore like to explain the hows and whys . . . for anyone who's interested.

The original idea for this book came from reading a book many years ago entitled *Stranger With My Face* by Lois Duncan. Prior to that time, I had never heard of the term "Astral Projection" nor had I ever heard of anyone having, or claiming to have, the ability to leave their bodies at will. I was particularly surprised to learn that certain groups of people, notably Indians in the Southwest, claimed to be able to teach and learn the art.

The idea stuck with me, and I pondered it on and off over the ensuing years. After all, who hasn't wondered sometime during their life what it would be like to be "a fly on the wall" and to be able to observe things otherwise not possible or permissible?

When I first entertained the idea of writing a novel, my goal and objective was to write a book that would be uplifting and enlightening to my readers—one that would inspire them to live betters lives as a result thereof.

Yet, at the same time, I wanted a book that would be captivating and interesting and fun to read. I refer to this type of wholesome entertainment as a "page-turning good time." And, in fact, the most common response I hear from my readers now is the phrase, "I just couldn't put it down." So I must have done something right along the way.

When I began searching for a topic, I was reminded of this unusual phenomenon of Astral Projection and decided to make it my central theme. My original outline for the first book was simple: 1) The protagonist discovers that he has the ability to leave his body at will, and 2) he uses his newfound ability to solve some sort of major crime. From there, the book just fell together, almost as fast as I could type.

But the fact remained that I really didn't know anything about Astral Projection beyond what I had read those many years ago in one solitary youth novel.

I realized that I needed to do some homework.

As I undertook my research, I made a number of startling discoveries. One was that there actually ARE many real people in the world who CAN leave their bodies at will. And many of them have already written books on the subject. I was fascinated to read of their out-of-body experiences and to learn about the things they saw and did in the spirit realms.

At first it was somewhat confusing. They all used their own phrases and terminology to describe their experiences, and I had a difficult time following them. But gradually I came to realize that they were all essentially saying the same thing. And when I overlaid their terminology with words that felt comfortable to me—from concepts that I had learned in my own religious upbringing— things became startlingly clear. It was like a revelation to me. I was truly entranced, and I yearned to know more.

Once I started visiting libraries, I discovered that nearly all books on the subject of Astral Projection were to be found on the same shelf as books about Palm Reading, ESP, Occultism, Shamanism, Black Magic, and various other paranormal topics. In fact, some of the Astral Projection books themselves mentioned or treated similar topics within their pages. This bothered me at first, because I had always related most of those sorts of things with Satan worship or other such bad doings. I certainly didn't want my books to portray "things evil." That would have defeated my entire purpose.

I thought a great deal on the subject, and finally concluded that perhaps none of those things were, in and of themselves, evil or bad. As I took a good long look around, I realized that virtually everything God has given us—be they talents and abilities, wisdom and intelligence, wealth and material possessions, or even inventions and technology—can all be used for either good or evil purposes, depending on the intentions of the individual. For instance, there's nothing inherently wrong with money—in and of itself. Yet MUCH good and MUCH evil have been accomplished with its use. The same can be said of virtually everything.

So I expanded my original goal and determined that I would portray the good that could come of someone endowed with this unusual ability. I deliberately avoided the use of any familiar terminology that might be interpreted as evil, and went to great lengths to depict my protagonist as a good person. I made it very clear, from the very beginning, that his ability WAS God given, and that it was intended to be used only for good.

Naturally I included a villain—a necessary element for a good book to achieve its end—and decided that he would be the exact opposite of my protagonist: someone who had learned or acquired the same ability, but had applied it to evil. The first two books in this series consist largely of the conflict between the two. In the end, the good wins.

And that's as it should be.

I have been richly rewarded with dozens and hundreds of fan letters and emails from people who had been "enlightened and uplifted, captivated and entertained" by my books. I've read many exuberant letters thanking me and sharing with me how my stories have inspired them or someone in their family—most notably teenagers and young adults who previously didn't have much of a desire to even read a book. I've been quite touched many times by tearful and emotional accounts of readers who have pledged to make their own lives better and to use their own gifts—whatever they might be—to the betterment of society.

And yet, still, there are some who would accuse me of advocating Satanism, promoting occultism, and dabbling in the forbidden and prohibited. I'm very sorry to have left that impression. It certainly was not my intention. I can only assume that their reasoning stems from a lack of understanding on their part concerning things spiritual, i.e. things beyond what we can see, hear, and touch in this limited, mortal existence.

Indeed, there is MUCH that we don't know. But there is much that we can learn. I would encourage those individuals to do some research of their own, and they will inevitably find what I have found: that the ability to leave one's body is a marvelous gift—one that almost always results in enhanced understanding, deeper wisdom, increased knowledge, and a clearer, more humble outlook on life—one that holds great potential for good, depending, of course, on the disposition of the gifted individual.

One final thought: It wasn't until later, after my books became widely distributed, that I made my most rewarding discovery. It turns out that there are actually people out there—people who have the gift—who don't know that it is, or can be, a good thing. They think they've been cursed. They live from day to day, minute to minute, ashamed of what they have, hiding it from their friends and family, or even trying to ignore or "undo" the gift. They didn't ask for it. It's just something they have, and they can't understand why they have it or what to do with it.

What a joy and a relief it is for them to discover and finally understand, through reading my books and others, that they aren't evil or condemned—to learn that what they have is really not bad at all. It's just a gift—like so many others enjoyed by the so-called "gifted and talented." It's how they use it that will ultimately determine its real worth.

I don't expect people to become super-spirit crime-solvers. That's the stuff good fiction is made of. But to hear of their resolve to share their gift and use it for good has brought me more fulfillment than I ever thought possible when I undertook this project.

And that's why I will continue the series, in spite of the criticism from the many "do-gooders" trying to "bring me to the light." I have seen too much good come of these books. And as it says in the scriptures, " . . . for every thing which inviteth to do good, and to persuade to believe in Christ, is sent forth by the power and gift of Christ: wherefore ye may know with a perfect knowledge it is of God."

My very ability to write is just such a gift, and I'm very grateful for it.

—Brent J. Rowley

Order Form

"The Perfect Gifts for Family and Friends"

To order additional, **autographed** copies of *Light Traveler Adventure Series,* send this form with a check or money order to:

Golden Wings Enterprises
P.O. Box 468
Orem, UT 84059-0468

Amount of Book 1 ordered _____ x $11.95 = $_____
(ISBN 0-9700103-1-1)

Amount of Book 2 ordered _____ x $12.95 = $_____
(ISBN 0-9700103-2-X)

Amount of Book 3 ordered _____ x $13.95 = $_____
(ISBN 0-9700103-3-8)

Sales Tax (add 6.25% for Utah addresses) $_____

Plus shipping and handling $ 2.00

Total $_____

Ship to:

Name _____

Address _____

City _____ State_____ ZIP_____

E-mail Address _____

Sending copies of this form is acceptable. Please allow three weeks for delivery. Prices good through December 31, 2001.

For fundraising, corporate, or reading club discounts, write to Golden Wings Enterprises, P.O. Box 468, Orem, UT 84059-0468